House of Matchsticks

PART ONE OF THE HOUSE OF MATCHSTICKS SERIES

ELISA DOWNING

This publication is a work of fiction. The names, characters, and events in this work are the products of the author's imagination and are used fictitiously. Any similarity to real persons living or dead is coincidental.

ISBN: 978-1-7773305-3-8 (Electronic Book)

ISBN: 978-1-7773305-2-1 (Paperback)

ISBN: 978-1-7773305-4-5 (Hardcover)

First edition, 2021

For content warnings, visit Elisa's website at elisadowning.com/content-warnings.

For Mom

You always lead me in the right direction.

BENEMOURNE
(East Side)
FORT UPPER
CASRET ACADEMY
LOWER VILLAGE
THE MILL
AR
N
W
E
S
THE SHUTE
SUNREST

TABLE OF CONTENTS

PRONUNCIATION GUIDE

Adrudian → a-DREW-dee-an
Agustin → Ah-GUST-in
Caladrius → cal-AH-dree-us
Fael → FYE-ell
Faraday → fair-AH-day
Isaline → ee-SAH-leen
Jame → JAY-m
Nalissa - nah-LISS-ah
Neave → NEEV
Purpesia → perp-EZ-ee-ah
Rhody → RO-dee
Shute → SHOOT

HOUSE OF MATCH STICKS

PART ONE OF THE HOUSE OF MATCHSTICKS SERIES

1

THE PUSH

THE COLLECTOR

Fire beckoned to the Collector as he walked over the sea.

Ahead, a starling fluttered on the salty breeze, black wings leading the Collector toward a bright spot of orange flame blooming on the horizon. He followed the bird with his eyes as she dipped and soared. She was darker than the night sky, a shadow flitting across gathering clouds and eluding what little moonlight shone through.

"Caladrius," the Collector called to her. "Slow down."

She made a turn in the air and chirped at him, impatient.

"It's not as if we'll be late," he said, but he hurried on all the same.

The fire took shape as they approached. The Collector held the brim of his hat between his fingers, craning to stare at the thick pillar of smoke rising into the sky. Hazy red light pushed the night's darkness back in all directions, save for Caladrius' figure flying up ahead. Her gliding silhouette swallowed the light, offering no reflection, giving the impression of a cutout shaped like a bird.

The Collector, too, was a cutout. His feet sank ankle-deep into the waves, dry despite the tossing water. He and Caladrius had been carved from the air with the same shears. Even to his own eyes, his body was nothing but a glittering, black shadow, filled with the winks of faraway stars.

He followed Caladrius until he stood a ship's length from the burning building, which sat atop a bare rock island. Squinting toward the blaze, the Collector pressed the pad of his thumb into the wire handle of his lantern, the Jar of Lights. The lantern's bright, sky-blue glow paled in the face of the inferno before them.

Caladrius circled back and settled onto the Collector's shoulder. The two of them stared awhile at the flames engulfing the building before the Collector said, "I wonder how hot it is inside."

The starling made no sound, just squeezed the fabric of his coat in her claws.

"It was a mill." The Collector lifted his gaze as a corner of the building's roof collapsed. "An Adrudian mill, wasn't it?"

The mill was a massive structure, tall and oblong, five

imposing stories of brick, wood, and metal. Dirty, barred windows lined the outside, many of them broken and shooting orange flames. The Collector spotted a pair of hands reaching through a shattered window, fingers gripped tight around the bars. A few seconds more and the hands slackened, falling, smoke billowing from where they disappeared.

Caladrius whistled and shifted from one foot to the other. The Collector shook his head, careful not to bump her.

"Not yet," he said.

Ahead of them, a handful of mill workers were huddled on the shore, holding the ends of their heavy aprons over their mouths and noses. One of them ushered the others toward the southern end of the island, where a slimy wooden dock extended over the sea. The Collector stood near the dock, next to a line of frail-looking rowboats bobbing in the water.

The mill workers rushed to the dock and stepped into the rowboats two at a time, unwinding the rope tethers. One pair rowed straight toward the Collector and Caladrius, heading for open water. The Collector, unfazed, stepped to the side to let the boat pass. He lifted the Jar of Lights above the mill workers' heads as they slid by, firelight glinting on their soot-streaked faces. Their gazes slipped over the Collector and Caladrius like river water over a rock.

When the boats had been reduced to specks in the

distance, the Collector nudged upwards with his shoulder to get Caladrius' attention. "One boat left."

The lone row boat drifted at the end of the dock, tethered to its post with a moldering rope. The Collector stared at its drifting frame, tiny against the hulk of the burning building. One rowboat couldn't carry the rest of the workers trapped inside the mill. There must have been hundreds working in a building this size.

Caladrius made a jittery sound and ruffled her wings. The Collector reached up and ran his hand gently down her back, letting her feathers smooth over his fingertips. He pressed his hat low onto his head.

"Okay. Let's go."

He made for the island, the blue glow from the Jar of Lights skating over the churning ocean. Caladrius was right; work needed to be done. She hopped from his shoulder and settled onto the brim of his hat, twittering as he walked.

The Collector had nearly reached the dock when the door of the mill slid open, startling him. He stopped with one foot extended as a woman appeared, stumbling out of the building in a hurry to escape the flames. She clutched a bundle to her chest, something wrapped in dirty white fabric. The Adrudian headlamp strapped over her forehead sent a beam of orange light bouncing off the smoke.

A pickaxer. The Collector set his foot down, toe dipping inside the water. She must have come up from the mines beneath the mill, where teams of pickaxers mined

Adrudian ore deep underground. He had assumed the pickaxers were trapped or dead.

The woman crossed the cracked concrete square in front of the mill and raced out onto the dock, her boots pounding on the slippery wood. Her overalls had been streaked with Adrudian Milk, the coppery, tacky liquid produced when the ore burned. Even the bundle clutched to her chest had been soaked with Milk, lines of brass-orange seeping into the center of the fabric.

"Do you think she swallowed any?" the Collector asked Caladrius, who had grown still on the brim of his hat.

Caladrius cooed in response. The Collector nodded. Of course, this woman hadn't swallowed any Adrudian Milk. She could still run, and the sweat-glistening, olive skin of her cheeks was clear of veins.

He drifted off to the side as the woman reached the end of the dock and stepped into the last rowboat. Breathing hard, she pulled the bundle from her chest, laid it across from her, and sat back to release the lines. The Collector looked into the boat and arched his brows. The bundle wasn't a pickaxe, as he had expected.

It was a child.

The baby stared upward, silent, eyes big in its face, while its mother pressed the boat's oars into their rowlocks. She rowed inexpertly away from the dock. The Collector peered at her smoke-burned eyes. They were brown, dark enough to reflect the flames in shades of orange. As she rowed, the woman glanced expectantly at the door of the mill, as if the fire could escape the building and chase after her. Caladrius' claws clenched the Collector's hat.

"Why do you think ..." the Collector started, but the words disappeared from his mouth as another person came bursting from the building: a man, clad in red, staggering through the door in a cloud of smoke. He charged over the ground so fast that he tripped and slid along the concrete. Like the mother in the boat, he had an Adrudian headlamp strapped to his forehead. Its orange beam waved as he rolled and got to his feet.

"*No,*" the mother screamed, making the Collector jump. Her face had twisted into a mask of horror, open-mouthed and wide-eyed. "Stay away from us, Johannes."

She rowed clumsily, trying to propel the boat through the water, but she didn't get far before the man called Johannes had lumbered toward her.

"I'm sorry," Johannes called out. His voice had a wet gurgle to it, as if he had swallowed swamp water. He jogged to the end of the dock and skidded to a stop, the toes of his boots hanging over the edge. "I really am sorry."

A cold feeling skittered up the Collector's spine. Johannes wasn't clad in red. He was soaked in damp, fresh blood. Crimson spread over him from the waist up, staining his shirt, streaking his face, mixing with coppery-orange splashes of Adrudian Milk. It was caked over his hands, solidifying in the spaces where his long, white fingers met his palms.

"Caladrius ..." the Collector murmured.

Johannes bared his teeth, yellow pearls shining out of blackened gums. "I didn't want this." He wiped the back of his hand across his dripping mouth, smearing red and brass-orange. "You chose this, didn't you?"

The mother's eyes filled with tears. The frail little rowboat couldn't move quick enough, or even at all, with the frantic way she pulled the oars.

"You chose this ... but *she* chose *me*. In the cave. In the House of Matchsticks," Johannes said. His eyes were blank, empty, the color of darkness. "I didn't have a choice."

The woman in the boat let the oars fall. They clattered against their wet rowlocks, and the child at the stern stirred inside its bundle. Its small hand broke free of the swaddle and waved in the air. Johannes looked from the baby to the mother, and back again.

"You can't save either of you by running, Theresa." His top lip curled into a sneer, streaks of blood flaking as they dried on his cheeks. "Come back here. Finish what we started, and she'll let you live. We'll be second only to gods."

Theresa shook her head, her shoulders trembling. Caladrius hopped down from the Collector's hat and onto his shoulder again. She whistled in his ear. Nodding, also feeling what was to come, the Collector slipped across the water to the rowboat.

"There are no gods. Not anymore. You've lost your mind," Theresa said. She reached behind her head and lifted a long, bronze chain from around her neck. A round pendant glinted at the end, about the size of a silver coin. It was made of a ruby-tinted stone the Collector didn't recognize with a center cutout in the shape of a keyhole. Johannes' gaze fixed on the pendant as Theresa pooled the chain in her palm.

"The keystone." Johannes swiped the back of his hand across his mouth a second time. "Think of what our friends went through, Theresa. Think of Mio, and Richard, and Haris. It was all for this."

Theresa shut her eyes, fresh tears spilling over her cheeks. Her hand closed around the pendant. "They're all dead."

"Richard still lives."

"That is no life." Sniffing, Theresa dropped the pendant into the heart of her baby's bundle. She tucked the waving arm back inside. "It's a mockery of life."

Johannes made a sound of such abrupt rage that the Collector flinched. "I *made* him. I saved him, and you're sabotaging everything we've worked for." His fingers twitched against his thighs. "*That* is the real abomination, Theresa."

But Theresa had stopped paying attention. She tenderly brushed her thumb over the baby's cheek, the space between her full brows knitting, eyes glassy in the light from the fire. Dread rose in Collector's chest as she folded the swaddle over the pendant, making sure it sat safely inside.

"You're going to get out of this," Theresa whispered to the child. "You're going to make your own choices and be so brave. I promise. I'll see it."

On the dock, Johannes snaked one of his blood-streaked hands behind his back. The muscles around his sunken eyes jumped, staring as Theresa pulled off her headlamp. Her long, ash brown hair hung in dirty clumps around her face.

"What are you doing?" Johannes demanded. The arm he had hidden behind his back quivered.

Theresa turned her rusty headlamp in her hands, the beam of orange Adrudian light shining over the boat's tiny interior. The Collector drifted closer as she took the bulb on the front of the headlamp and, in one sharp movement, smashed it against the side of the boat. The bulb cracked and shattered. Shards of glass splashed into the sea.

Johannes groaned, a sound that bubbled in the back of his throat like hot oil. "No, Theresa, don't ..."

She tipped the headlamp, shaking the loose rock of Adrudian behind the broken bulb into her cupped hand. The Adrudian glowed like a tiny orange star, oozing Adrudian Milk from its porous exterior. Liquid puddled in Theresa's palm.

"*Theresa, no,*" Johannes cried, and two things

happened at once: Johannes pulled his hand out from behind his back, revealing a long pistol, and Theresa tilted her head and swallowed the Adrudian ore and the Milk all in one.

The Collector grimaced, spine straightening as Theresa's eyes rolled and clamped shut. Her face contorted, mouth dropping open. Midnight-blue veins popped out of the sides of her cheeks, climbing like vines from her throat to the corners of her eyes.

Johannes groaned again. His arm shook so fiercely that he almost dropped his pistol into the water. "Your face, Theresa ..." He raised and lowered the gun, fighting with himself, while Theresa collapsed against the bow of the boat. Her eyes shifted rapidly beneath her eyelids, deep in the powerful vision brought to her by the Adrudian Milk in her bloodstream. "Your *face* ..."

The Collector studied Theresa's swinging eyes. Was she lucky enough to have the vision she wanted to see—her child escaping this place, growing old, making choices, and being brave? Or did the Adrudian bring her only seconds into the future, granting her the sight of Johannes cocking the pistol, seconds before he really did?

It made no difference. She would never surface from this vision. Johannes pulled the trigger on his pistol and shot her in the chest.

Dark blood bloomed over Theresa's body, soaking her pickaxer's overalls. Stains spread like flowers. Cringing, the Collector adjusted his grip on the Jar of Lights.

Caladrius twittered, tipping her head side-to-side as air leaked from Theresa's mouth, long and slow.

On the dock, Johannes moaned, his face obscured by curls of smoke billowing from the barrel of his gun. He hung his head, chin resting on his chest, then looked up at the boat again. It floated, hardly moving, the baby bundle sitting at its end.

The Collector flicked his eyes at Caladrius. "Is he going to ...?"

Johannes' eyes went bright with rage. He cocked the pistol mechanically, as if out of control of himself. He aimed the gun at the baby bundle. Ice crept into the Collector's veins, and he braced himself for the shot to ring out, cracking the air.

There was no crack. When the shot came, it sounded like a shot fired from a canon rather than a pistol.

The gun backfired. Its grip blew open, sending red-hot Adrudian and fire tearing into Johannes' chest and face. There was no time for him to scream. He fell in a cloud of smoke, the force of the blast propelling his now detached hand—still clutching the shredded pistol grip—into the water.

Stillness fell. The Collector's fingertips prickled the way they did when a human was close to death. Caladrius made no sound, just stared at Johannes' body bleeding on the dock. His face and chest were ripped apart. The Collector glanced at her on his shoulder.

"Is he dead, Cal? Dying?"

She whistled low and long. *No* to both questions. The hair on the back of the Collector's neck rose. He had seen deaths, thousands of them, but had never seen a human survive such a wound.

Swallowing, he dragged his eyes from Johannes and walked to the little rowboat. He peered over the side. Theresa's body slumped, chin lolling on her chest, blood dripping from her fingertips. The baby wriggled in its bundle and turned its eyes up to the sky. The Collector stared at it, fiddling with the brim of his hat.

Caladrius chirped at him.

"Yes, I guess ..." The Collector hesitated. Something about the baby's face made his words stick in his throat. "I guess let's do it, then."

He changed his composition and sank into the water up to his waist. The Jar of Lights, hanging from the crook of his elbow, shone a bright circle of blue around them. The Collector reached into the boat and pushed a strand of hair from Theresa's face. Her eyes were still, seeing nothing. He turned her head gently, examining the blue veins climbing her cheeks.

The Collector had seen Adrudian Drinkers before, but he had never grown accustomed to their faces swollen with poison. Even alive, Drinkers were ghosts, both plagued and blessed with the visions Adrudian Milk gifted them.

As he released her, a mark on the side of Theresa's neck caught the Collector's eye. He brushed a lock of brown hair from her shoulder. Was it a bruise? No—a tattoo. The lines were rudimentary, as if inscribed by an untrained hand, but the design was unmistakable. Three squares overlaid on top of each other, lines intersecting the pattern at top and bottom, left and right.

The Collector blinked. Where had he seen this symbol before?

Caladrius landed on Theresa's chest, her claws making no indent in the bloody fabric of the pickaxer's overalls. She gazed up at the Collector.

"Okay," he said, letting Theresa's hair fall back over the tattoo.

She hopped into the air again, settling on the top of his head, and gripped the stiff fabric of his hat as he bent over the side of the rowboat. The Collector laid his hand on Theresa's chest and *pulled,* like he had done countless times before, not so much with his body as with his mind. Light pooled beneath the palm of his hand.

A person's soul gleamed like bright smoke. Smoke only the Collector's hands could catch.

He led Theresa's soul into the Jar of Lights. It bobbed and circled inside the lantern, an orb of brilliant white light. The Collector watched it settle with the other orbs swirling there, others that hadn't seen fit to leave this world quite yet.

As the Collector stood, his job done, the baby made a quiet burble. He turned his head and stared at the bundle sitting at the stern of the boat.

"How is it not crying?" he asked Caladrius.

She fluttered down from his hat to perch on the edge of the rowboat, looking from him to the baby. The Collector ran a hand over his jaw.

"It's just ... odd."

Behind them, the mill's roof finally collapsed, sending fire and smoke soaring into the sky. The Collector studied the roof as it fell, an uneasy feeling gathering in his gut. By the time the sun rose, there would be nothing left. There would be no Adrudian mill, and—he could feel it in his fingertips—there would be no more survivors. None, except for Johannes, perhaps, whose destroyed body still somehow breathed on the dock.

Johannes, and this small one he had tried to kill.

The Collector looked at the baby. It smacked its lips, screwing up its face and opening its eyes to the sky, looking on with wonder at stars hidden behind smoke. The Collector didn't know how it felt to be young, or to be human—to see the world come alive with mysteries. His purpose as Death was simple: he collected the souls of humans and carried them until they left, rising from the Jar of Lights and flying somewhere beyond the stars. Someone like him wasn't meant to be curious, or to open his eyes to the sky and wonder.

Standing by the rowboat, the Collector followed the baby's gaze and looked up. Then he glanced out over the dark sea, in the direction he knew would lead to land, and a village. It was a small village, but populated, sitting at the edge of one of the largest train stations west of the mountains.

A person could go almost anywhere if they caught a train from that station.

He stared, chewing on his lip. The baby blew air out of its mouth in a tiny sigh. The Collector smiled, imagining what it would feel like to take a breath, to let the sea air fill his lungs.

On impulse, he reached out, put his hand on the boat, and gave it a little push. Not a big one, but just enough—just enough to send it in the direction of that village. A dark shadow spread out onto the wood, unfurling like glittering black ink in water, and the boat lurched with a splash. The Collector's stomach flipped, fearing that he had unwittingly performed some dark magic, but as his fingertips left the wood, the glittering shadow receded, and the boat returned to normal.

Caladrius sang and touched down on his shoulder, her claws squeezing. They stayed still for a long time, watching the boat drift over the waves, carrying the bundle and its dead mother with it.

"Well, there it goes," the Collector said. The sound of his own voice seemed strange to him, but Caladrius chirped warmly, rubbing the top of her head against his chin. She leaped off his shoulder and flew toward the island, beckoning for him to follow.

He nodded at her. Turning, he spared one last look over the sea, to where the ripple of water from that small rowboat would reach across years and become a wave. The Collector didn't see the wave—all he saw was a boat washing into the distance, a rocky island peppered with the dead, and a bird, flying like light's opposite toward a great inferno, leading him on.

In the end, the Collector thought, almost as a comfort, *all will be Collected.*

He shifted his grip on the Jar of Lights and walked to the burning mill, his hat sitting low on his head.

2

SIXTEEN YEARS LATER

ISALINE

On the night before her Weeklong Review, Isaline returned to her dorm room to find that her best friend had been snooping through her bureau.

Isaline's fingers slid off the top drawer as she examined the arrangement of items inside. The bureau was made of old pine, crisscrossed with deep scratches, a relic of Casret Watch Academy's early days. Isaline's few possessions barely filled its three drawers.

Still, something was off. Things weren't as she left them: Isaline's comb was turned on its side, her umber curls spilling from its teeth; her copy of the City Watch oath was crumpled; the hand mirror she'd bought in Fort Upper was pushed into the wrong corner. Strangest of all, her jewelry box was missing.

Closing the drawer, Isaline spun slowly on the spot, her eyes running over everything in her tiny, shared room. Two beds with gray coverlets sat parallel against opposite walls, flanked by desks and bureaus. A tall, recessed window divided the space between the two beds, separating the room into halves. Midnight pressed its dark face against the window panes.

Isaline crossed to her writing desk and turned the dial on her lantern. A slat opened at the bottom of the lantern's glass bulb, letting light escape from the Adrudian ore within. The room brightened, and Isaline spotted her missing jewelry box sitting half-hidden under a pile of papers on Nalissa's desk.

A bumping sound came from the bathroom, startling her. Nalissa was here after all. Holding her breath, Isaline tipped her ear toward the noise. There it was again—the telltale sound of a drawer closing.

Isaline wanted to call out, but her voice hid in the back of her throat. She and Nalissa had been roommates and best friends for five years; why would Nalissa be going through her things in secret?

Another drawer in the bathroom closed. Isaline glanced at the jewelry box on Nalissa's desk and tucked the pendant hanging around her neck into the collar of her shirt. It was a good thing she had decided to wear the pendant to the library tonight.

For now, Isaline left the jewelry box where it was and

shrugged off her overcoat. She changed quickly into her nightclothes, suppressing a series of gasps. Her muscles ached from the long days she had spent practicing for the Weapons Portion of her Weeklong Review.

Leaving her school uniform on the floor, she sat down on her bed, stretching her shoulders. The old, rusted springs of her mattress creaked, and the knocking sounds behind the bathroom door came to an abrupt stop. Her stomach worked itself into a knot. Nalissa had left evidence of her snooping everywhere. She obviously hadn't been expecting Isaline back so soon.

The bathroom door cracked open and Nalissa's head emerged.

"You're back early." Her hair, brown and longer than Isaline's, was tied up in a knot at the base of her neck. She smiled a little too widely, and her voice was a little too high.

"I gave up studying," Isaline said. She rubbed the soreness out of the tops of her thighs with her hands, suppressing another gasp. "The words were all running together."

"They'll do that. Turn the textbook upside down next time, that'll shake them loose." Nalissa walked stiffly from the bathroom and leaned on her writing desk, blocking Isaline's view of the jewelry box with her hips. "You feel prepared for the Survival Portion?"

Isaline gave her a look. Nalissa snorted.

"Typical. You're going to regret not studying for the Survival Portion one day, you know."

"It's not for lack of trying," Isaline said. She had spent the evening hunched over her textbooks in the Academy's library, mindlessly flipping through pages on fire-building and rabbit-snaring. It was no use. She wasn't a survivalist like Nalissa—but Nalissa seemed to be a natural at everything.

"You look sore, too," Nalissa said. Her dark eyes were keen and awake, watching Isaline closely despite the late hour. "Maybe you should reschedule. Go out some other week."

Isaline shrugged, taking the opportunity to work her fingers into the muscles under her shoulder blades. "You and I already switched weeks. Waiting won't make me better at Country Watch stuff. Might as well get it over with."

Nalissa tapped her fingertips, something she did when she was nervous. A bracelet—not Isaline's—hung around her wrist, purple beads complementing her fawn complexion. "I mean ..." She shifted. The corner of Isaline's jewelry box was just visible beyond her side. "Maybe you should reschedule anyway. There have been rumors about the training area, you know."

"What? About the guy that's out there?"

Nalissa nodded. "Only ... Marik Taylor said it didn't look much like a guy."

Isaline worked her hand into the bottom of her foot.

She winced as the muscles smarted under her touch. "He was trying to impress you, though. Marik told you he saw a monster on his Weeklong last year, too, remember? It turned out to be a squirrel."

"Right, but then there's those missing guards."

"Missing," Isaline said, "or getting drunk in Fort Upper?"

Nalissa turned to the window, staring over the dark, sprawling forest that comprised Casret Academy's training area. West of the forest stood the small city of Fort Upper, the favorite drinking refuge of the Academy guards that manned the training area at outposts. They pulled double duty this time of year when the Academy sent students into the forest for the Survival Portion of their Weeklong Reviews, but it was common knowledge they took long drink breaks.

"Why are you so worried?" Isaline shifted on her bed, scooting up to her pillows. "I'm going to pass the Weapons Portion, so the Survival Portion isn't going to matter. I can trigger the flare on day one and still pass. Really, the worst that's going to happen is I forget which grass to eat."

Nalissa fidgeted, angling her body to keep the jewelry box out of Isaline's sightline. She broke into a smile that was a little tense at the edges. "You shouldn't actually eat grass."

"Berries, then." Isaline looked her in the eye and Nalissa's smile pulled back even more. "It'll be fine. If I come across some weird drifter, I'll just kill him."

A laugh burst out of Nalissa's mouth, the first genuine sound she'd made tonight. Isaline lifted the thin coverlet on her bed and tucked herself beneath it. Nalissa wasn't going to bring up the jewelry box, that was clear. Isaline would have to goad her into it somehow.

"So ..." Isaline blew out her cheeks, then released the air with a little *pop*. "What did you get up to tonight?"

Nalissa raised her hands, a noncommittal gesture that wrapped Isaline's stomach into a knot again. "Studied."

"You practice your oath?"

Her face slipped, but returned to normal so fast Isaline couldn't catch her expression. "No, I—I haven't yet."

"You should get on it, Country Watchling." Isaline yawned, keeping one eye slit open. "You'll be going into the forest after I get out, which—if I'm honest—means we'll be taking our oaths at graduation soon."

Nalissa nodded, and kept nodding so that her head resembled a daffodil bobbing silently in the wind. Isaline pulled the coverlet up to her chin and tried to dampen the worried flame growing in her middle. Nalissa had a reputation for talking—even the Academy's professors had commented on how loquacious she could be—but tonight it seemed she had little to say.

"Well, goodnight." Isaline rubbed her eyes and turned over to face the wall. If Nalissa didn't want to talk, there would be no conversation tonight; on a good day, Isaline had only one or two words for Nalissa's ten, and none of them were brave enough to start a confrontation. "See you in the morning."

Nalissa mumbled something in response, then reached out and turned down the dial on the lantern, filling the room with darkness.

The next morning, Isaline opened her eyes to sunlight streaming in through the window. Nalissa had gone downstairs for breakfast, and the jewelry box had been returned, tucked perfectly inside Isaline's top drawer as if it had never left.

Isaline hurried across Casret Academy's grassy courtyard, her black canvas bag bumping her hip. A few students milled around, but not many. Most had finished their Weeklongs and left the Academy for summer vacation, leaving campus emptier than usual.

As Isaline walked, she reached up to her neck and tucked her red keyhole pendant into the front of her top. She prayed to whoever had given it to her, asking for luck. Isaline wasn't sure they listened, but in four years of Weeklongs she had never eaten a poison mushroom, and for that she was willing to believe.

Like the courtyard, Casret's cafeteria was close to empty. The few students who had come for breakfast were all gathered at one table, talking excitedly about summer vacation. Isaline helped herself to a plate of the biggest pancakes at the buffet and nodded to the short, grizzled man behind the counter.

"Morning," she said.

He smiled at her, his thin beard gathering at his cheeks. "Last Weeklong Review starting today?"

Isaline was already chewing, so she just nodded. He passed another pancake onto her plate and winked.

"Good luck," he said. "There's a lot on the line."

There was. The Weeklong Review was high-stakes, especially in a student's final year. Luckily for Isaline, a student only had to pass one portion of the exam—the Weapons Portion or the Survival Portion—in order to pass the entire thing. She was a good fighter, so aside from graduation jitters, her nerves were as quiet as midnight. She thanked him and walked over to Nalissa, who waved at her from their usual spot under a stained-glass window.

Five or six students Isaline didn't know were sitting at their table, talking among themselves and casting sidelong glances at Nalissa, who sat quietly staring into space. The flame of worry in Isaline's middle sparked to life again. She was used to seeing Nalissa in animated conversation with one or two of her admirers—other students that followed Nalissa everywhere, trying to befriend her. Today, Nalissa didn't speak until Isaline dropped into the empty seat beside her.

"You know the Weapons Portion comes first, right?" she said, eyeing Isaline's pancakes.

Isaline was already halfway through the second. "Pancakes make me a better fighter. It's been proven with years of testing."

Nalissa laughed but didn't offer another response. Instead, she gazed across the cafeteria, drumming her fingers on the tabletop. Her hair was bound in its usual knot, this time sitting at the crown of her head like the round petals of a flower. On days like today, when they were both in uniform, she could have been Isaline's sister. Both Isaline and Nalissa had strong brows and square jaws, though Isaline's chin tapered into a small cleft where Nalissa's was rounded. Talkativeness, Isaline supposed, was what truly set them apart—though that didn't seem to be the case this morning.

Isaline stuck another forkful of food in her mouth, waiting for Nalissa to continue the conversation. She didn't.

"Sleep well?" Isaline asked.

"Sure." Nalissa's eyes rested on Isaline and flew away again, like a moth that couldn't decide where to land. "Not for very long. But I feel ... rested."

Isaline chewed, narrowing her eyes. Nalissa had always been an early riser, a practice that made her an ideal candidate for Country Watch. As a student preparing for a life in the City Watch, Isaline treasured her sleep. She'd need it during her days patrolling and keeping Benemourne's urban districts safe, especially if she got stationed in Ar, Benemourne's capital and Isaline's dream city.

"You didn't ..." Isaline pressed her lips together. Being friends with Nalissa, she'd never had to be the articulate one. "You didn't have anything you wanted to talk about?"

The corners of Nalissa's mouth turned downward in a frown so exaggerated it made Isaline's eyebrows arch. "No, what do you mean?"

"You've been acting ... well, odd," Isaline said. She added a shrug to make it seem like less of an accusation.

The other students at the table quieted, clearly listening. Isaline's fork nearly slipped from her hand. For her, having any conversation felt like navigating an obstacle course; doing so with Nalissa while a legion of her admirers watched was like running through a pitch-black maze filled with traps.

Nalissa blinked, her downturned mouth hiding a glimmer of a secret. "Odd? How?"

Isaline squeezed her eyes shut. Words wouldn't come out of her mouth if she kept looking Nalissa in the face. "Our room was ... a little messy when I came back last night." She cracked one eye open. A look of such panic had crossed Nalissa's face that Isaline's heart thumped. She swerved. "The papers on your desk. You've been writing a lot of letters."

The look of panic subsided. "It's not—not anything important. They're just letters."

"Letters? To *who*?" a male voice said.

Marik Taylor slid into the open seat next to Isaline. He propped his elbow on the tabletop and loosened his tie, tugging it from his collar. "Who do you have to write letters to?" he asked again. His right incisor was gold, sparkling as he flashed Nalissa a wide smile. "I thought you didn't know anyone outside the Academy."

Isaline kicked him under the table. Marik recoiled, grunting.

"It's just a question," he said.

"A stupid question," Isaline replied. Outside Casret, she and Nalissa were both placeless—people without families or homes to visit. Nalissa and Isaline's friendship had grown partly from this shared reliance, the knowledge they had no one else but each other.

At the beginning, anyway, Isaline corrected herself. These days, Nalissa had attention and support wherever she went, her future as a brilliant member of the Country Watch solidified by her skill and excellent graduating marks. Isaline could think of no one more deserving. Still, Nalissa struggled not knowing where she was from, and Marik's senses were too dull to intuit that all on his own.

"If you keep kicking people, you'll never get a spot in Ar, you know." Marik's eyes sparkled, giving his gold tooth something to contend with. His goading was harmless, but Isaline had to hide a pinch that formed in her chest. "Speaking of which ... heading out today, then?"

Isaline returned to her pancakes. "Oh good, you're here to tell me about the squirrel you saw in the forest."

"Not a squirrel." Marik reached his hand toward her

plate, grabbing for her last pancake. She smacked his fingers with her fork. "It was something *else*."

A ripple went through the students sitting at the table, including Nalissa. Isaline cut down into her pancake hard enough for her knife to squeak on her plate. "Something else like a raccoon?"

Nalissa chuckled, followed by a chorus of laughter from the other students. The tip of Marik's nose reddened. Isaline waved her fork in the air.

"Just kidding, Marik. Go on."

Marik swiveled in his seat so he was facing Nalissa and Isaline head-on. He rubbed his hands together. "I saw it at night, so I didn't get the greatest look. It was curled up on a rock, kind of like a sleeping snake, you know? But it was shaped like a man."

Isaline couldn't picture a sleeping-man-shaped snake on a rock, but the other students obviously could. They let out a series of *oohs*.

Emboldened, Marik leaned toward Isaline until she could see every hair in his tiny mustache. "It was wearing some kind of white robe."

"What did it do?" Nalissa asked, her voice hushed.

Marik grinned at her over Isaline's shoulder. "It moved. It kind of coiled over, like it was going to do a somersault, right? It spread out on its belly. Then—" He smacked his palm on the tabletop, making the students jump. "It slithered away through the forest."

"Did you see its face?" one of the other students asked.

His eyes were round enough to hide two pieces of silver behind.

Marik rubbed a hand over his jaw. “Sort of. It could have looked like a human, I guess. Except for the eyes.” He looked around to all of them, an angled smile inching across his face. “There was something wrong with the eyes.”

Isaline turned to Nalissa, expecting to pass a look of disbelief between them, but her face was drawn and nervous. Marik crossed his arms, soaking up the students’ second round of *oohs* and *aahs*.

“So, to sum up,” Isaline said, “you saw a guy lying face down on a rock wearing his nightclothes.”

Marik pulled his gaze from Nalissa to glower at Isaline. “Not *that* kind of robe.”

“I think it sounds scary,” Nalissa volunteered. The other students nodded, and kept nodding for a few beats too long, just like Nalissa always did. Isaline suppressed an eye roll so severe she could have seen the back of her head.

“All right, it sounds a little creepy,” Isaline said. “Thanks for saying something.”

Marik nodded, sliding out of his seat. He tried to pat Isaline on the shoulder, but she blocked his hand, so he ended up patting her forearm instead. “Good luck out there, City Watchling,” he said. Smiling, he gave Nalissa a two-finger salute. “See you later.”

“Bye,” Nalissa said. The tips of her ears deepened to a

flushed red.

When Marik had disappeared from the cafeteria, Isaline shot Nalissa a look. "Why don't you just ask him out, so next time he won't have to make up a monster to talk to you? I'm going through a lot, over here."

Nalissa shoved Isaline's arm. "I don't like him like that!"

"Tell that to your face."

They laughed, Nalissa with her mouth hidden behind her hand, then smiled at each other. Isaline glanced out the window.

"Hey," she said. "We'll talk when I get back, okay? I have a date with a sparring clockwork."

Nalissa took a long breath, as if it were the last free breath she'd ever take. "Okay." She squeezed Isaline's shoulder. "Go disarm that clockwork. And don't eat anything you shouldn't during the Survival Portion."

"No promises."

Isaline stood up, trying to be gentle on her aching muscles, and hurried out of the cafeteria toward the first part of her exam. The flame of worry in her stomach burned fresh and strong. She could feel Nalissa's eyes following her all the way.

Isaline burst into the Academy's training center a full minute behind schedule. The double doors slammed behind her as she sprinted into the examination arena, cursing herself for not outright asking Nalissa about the jewelry box. On her way to the training center, she had nearly turned back to the cafeteria twice. The indecision had made her late.

"I'm here!" Isaline announced, skidding to a stop on the sparring floor.

The examiners, a group of five men and women standing high up on the arena's observation deck, said nothing. The Headmaster of Casret Academy was standing in the middle of the group, his eyes hidden behind the glare on his round spectacles.

Isaline swore under her breath. She wished Nalissa had waited until *after* her Weeklong to keep secrets.

Casret's examining arena was an old, mahogany-paneled room. The observation deck looked out over a spread of black, padded floor with a big red X in the center. Along the walls, a multitude of weapons hung on hooks and sat on shelves. Isaline spotted her favorite trident hanging up along the far wall, and a surge of adrenaline washed through her, easing some of the soreness in her muscles.

The Headmaster glanced down at the clipboard in his hands.

"City Watch?" he asked. His voice had a bored drawl to it, implying he had other, more exciting places to be.

Isaline walked into the center of the red X. "Yes."

"I have Country Watch listed here," the Headmaster

said, as if the error were Isaline's fault. He scratched something out on his clipboard. "The examination will proceed."

Isaline pulled off her coat and tossed it to the edge of the sparring floor with her bag. A woman she didn't recognize stepped forward from the line of examiners.

"The Weapons Portion of the Weeklong Review has now begun," she said. Her voice was silky, the kind of voice Isaline wouldn't have associated with a member of the Watch. "Choose from the first weapon group, please."

Isaline turned to the wall at her right. A large number one was emblazoned across it in white paint. The weapons lined up along this wall were all blades, large and small. She selected a worn short sword and returned to the center of the room.

"The Weapons Portion is made up of four sparring sections," the silky-voiced woman said. Isaline squinted up to the observation deck, but the woman's face was hidden behind the glow of an Adrudian lantern. "Each section lasts sixty seconds. The goal in each section is to disarm the clockwork. If the student fails to disarm the clockwork, but they still have their own weapon, they will receive partial marks for that section. If the student is disarmed by the clockwork at any point during the exam, the student fails the Weapons Portion."

Isaline shifted her grip on the sword and shook out her arms, ignoring the pain in her muscles. She had forfeited her chance to warm up by arriving late. "Let's go, then."

With a loud whirring sound, a portion of the floor slid open a few feet in front of her, revealing a square hole. Isaline peered into the darkness as a platform ascended, carrying an Academy-issue sparring clockwork.

Looking at it, Isaline's gut squirmed. The clockwork wasn't particularly tall, but it was bulky, man-shaped, and had a broad chest like a boulder. Wood, rubber, and brass interlinked its joints. At the end of one arm hung a deadly iron sword, held protectively over a plate-sized patch of orange Adrudian in its belly. Isaline held her breath, trying not to look at the clockwork's head, which was just a smooth, round sheet of wood. It had no eyes or ears, but it *sensed* her, in the ghostly way all the King's inventions did.

"Begin," the silky-voiced examiner said.

The clockwork sprang forward, bringing its sword up in attack position. Isaline had a split second to bring her own sword up in defense before it hit her head-on with incredible strength and knocked her backward. She landed hard on her backside, the jolt rocking her spine to the top of her ribs.

Is this a joke? Isaline stared open-mouthed at the clockwork as it stretched its arms. It was stronger than it looked—*way* too strong for one Watchling to take on alone.

Her stomach dropped as the clockwork lunged again. Isaline rolled to the left, tucking the short sword. The clockwork's feet landed with a rib-rattling *thud* on the mat. She scrambled to stand.

The next sixty seconds blurred. The clockwork struck

again and again, and even when Isaline attempted to parry the attack, the sheer force of the machine sent her flying. Over the course of the whole fight, she got five attacks of her own in, two of which made contact. By the time the examiners rang the bell to signal the end of the section, she had taken two chunks of rubber out of the top of the clockwork's left arm, but had nothing to show for the fight except her own bruised backside and a swollen lip.

"Partial marks," the examiner said. "Please choose from the second weapon group."

The clockwork returned to its original position. Isaline took a few seconds to catch her breath, then peeled herself off the floor and returned the short sword to the wall. Her chest was on fire. How did *anyone* pass this year, with that clockwork as their sparring partner? She glanced up at the examiners and was met with the stony face of the Headmaster watching her every move. Maybe this *was* the test; the examiners wanted to see if she would give up.

The second weapon group was made up of blunt weapons. Isaline chose a two-handed hammer, heaved it from the wall, and, at the examiner's command, the clockwork attacked again.

By the time Isaline had reached the fourth and last weapon group, her skin was mottled with bruises and oozing cuts. Her body pulsed painfully as she dragged herself to standing. She had not yet lost her weapon to the clockwork—which meant she had not failed—but there were moments where it had been close. She pulled the back of her arm across her mouth, smearing blood from her split lip.

The clockwork stood in its starting position. She had managed to make a small dent in one of its thighs with the hammer, and there were a few punctures in its chest from the flail she had used in the third section, but otherwise it was untouched.

"Partial marks," the examiner said. "Please choose from the fourth weapon group. This is your final chance to disarm the clockwork and achieve one round of full marks."

Isaline suppressed an upward glare before turning to the fourth and final wall. There, hanging beneath the dripping paint of the emblazoned number four, was her favorite trident. Isaline's heart leaped. The trident was her best weapon. She had even won a spar against Nalissa with it once, a feat that Casret's best students couldn't boast.

Stepping up to the wall, Isaline wrapped her fingers around the trident's staff and pulled it down. Collapsed, the spear was short, about the length of her torso. Isaline held the trident out and pressed the button on the middle grip. The staff extended smoothly on both ends to its full length. Her heart fluttered as three razor-sharp points slid out the top and clicked into place.

The world seemed to tilt right-side up again. The clockwork had proven impossible to overcome; it was ten times stronger than it looked, and it looked like it could uproot an oak tree. Fighting such a powerful machine had forced Isaline to stay on the defensive, riding out the sixty seconds until the bell rang. But with the trident, maybe she *could* disarm it for full marks. The Head Inspector in Ar would surely hire her with the highest Weapons Portion marks in her class.

She returned to the center of the red X. Bending her knees, she lowered her center of gravity and raised the trident. Her fingers tightened on the strong metal.

"Ready," she said under her breath.

"Begin," came the examiner's voice. The clockwork jolted to life.

Isaline was prepared this time. As the clockwork came at her with the sword, she feinted left and struck out with the staff of the trident. It *thwacked* against the clockwork's wooden arm and the machine lurched to the side.

Isaline's heart hammered against her ribs. She pulled the trident back and bent her knees.

Focus.

The clockwork turned, arcing its sword at the top of her head. Isaline stepped to the right, dodged the blow, and extended the trident out and under the clockwork's sword arm. She thrust it upward, trying to knock the sword out of its hand. The staff smacked against the clockwork's arm, but the sword didn't budge.

Get back, she coached herself. *Give it some distance.*

Isaline retracted the spear and rushed backward. The clockwork turned its huge, blank face and ran at her like a battering ram, sword extended. Isaline feinted again, to the right this time, and brought the trident down in a wide sweep. The clockwork didn't have time to react. The spear hit it above the ankles, sending it sprawling in a heap.

Every inch of Isaline's skin tightened. This was her chance. She adjusted her grip on the spear and lifted it over her head. Rushing forward, she aimed the trident's three shiny points at the clockwork's back. It was the same tactic she'd used in her spar with Nalissa. As she ran, a memory surfaced: Isaline recreating the spar move-by-move while Nalissa leaned, laughing, against her desk.

The same desk that had held Isaline's jewelry box.

The image distracted Isaline for less than a second, but it was enough time for the clockwork to roll aside. Isaline cried out, an involuntary sound of surprise. She tried to correct her movement, but there was too much momentum behind the blow—she lost her footing and stumbled. The point of the trident stuck into the floor, a third of the length of its prongs disappearing into the mat. The staff was wrenched out of Isaline's hands, and she fell straight onto the clockwork. Air burst out of her mouth, flattening her chest.

The clockwork rose beneath her and shook her off as if she were weightless. She went rolling across the mat and onto all fours, gasping. The clockwork got to its feet and plucked the trident out of the mat, lifting it over its head.

"That's enough," the Headmaster said, and the clockwork stilled.

Isaline's lungs had shrunk to the size of pebbles. She locked her elbows so she wouldn't fall face-first into the mat.

The woman examiner's voice rang out around the arena. "Fail."

A sick feeling washed through Isaline. This had to be a mistake. *No one* could take down that clockwork.

The Headmaster tucked his clipboard under his arm and peered down through his spectacles.

"Such a shame." He tutted, shaking his head. "A fight clearly unworthy of a place in Ar."

It was the worst thing he could have said to an aspiring City Watch. Isaline tried to reply, but her voice came out a croak. Sweat stung her eyes.

"The Weapons Portion of the Weeklong Review has now ended," the woman examiner said. Her face was still hidden behind the nimbus of the Adrudian lantern. "Please change into the appropriate clothes and lock your belongings in the designated chests. We will brief you once you are ready to proceed out of the back doors of the Training Center and into the forest. The Survival Portion begins now."

The woman pressed a button on the control box beside her. A clockwork mechanism *clunked*, and a pair of double doors beneath the observation deck swung open, letting in a blast of sunlight. Isaline shaded her eyes.

Wait, she wanted to say. *Wait, give me another chance.*

But when her eyes adjusted to the light, she lowered her arm to find that the observation deck was empty, and the examiners were gone.

3

THE EXECUTION OF THE JUSTS

THE COLLECTOR

It was midday, blazing hot. The Collector and Caladrius made their way through the shimmering brick streets of Ar on their way to the palace square.

Caladrius flitted through iron railings and skimmed over lengths of colored fabric drying in the heat. The Collector trailed after her, hiking up Ar's sloping roads. The city was built on the side of a mountain, a tiered and vertical metropolis connected by winding streets and alleys. Traveling from Ar's base to its peak meant a two-day excursion through the cramped and greasy city, or a slightly shorter trolley ride. The Collector walked. He'd never done anything else.

Keeping Caladrius in sight, the Collector rounded a bend onto a narrow street. He sidestepped past a rumpled-looking merchant leaning close to another woman.

"He's caught them," she whispered. "The King's finally caught them."

The same whisper was spreading through the crowd, growing in volume as they got closer to the palace. Word had gotten around about the public execution being held this afternoon.

The crush of people heading to the palace square thickened until the Collector was forced to pass spectrally through them. He gritted his teeth and melted through their bodies, trying not to focus on how it felt. Humans made his movements sluggish, like he was trudging through knee-deep mud.

"I heard the King didn't have to hunt them down," a man said to his neighbor as the Collector passed through their shoulders. "They surrendered themselves to the City Watch. They just walked up to the Watch Wall with their hands—"

The rest of his sentence was drowned out by the drumming engine of a white-ballooned airship. The Collector looked up, slowing his pace as the crowd gazed at the machine ascending the side of the mountain. Seeing an airship was rare these days. Benemourne's former rulers, the Seven Thrones, had commissioned a fleet of them to transport people around Ar, but most of the airships had been discontinued since the overthrow.

"Caladrius," the Collector called, taking advantage of the pause. The crowd's insides were sticky, gripping his spine. He gestured to the buildings on either side of the street. "I can't get through like this. I'm going up."

Caladrius chirped, circling around while the Collector hooked the Jar of Lights over his elbow and trudged to the nearest building. There, he sidestepped a group of blue-veined Adrudian Drinkers huddled behind a makeshift stand, climbed a stretch of iron lattice, and pulled himself over the edge of the roof.

On one side, the mumbling crowd rolled beneath him like a multicolored river. On the other, tiers of red-tiled rooftops led to the bottom of the mountain, coming up against the huge, white-marbled arches of Ar's Watch Wall. Beyond the Wall, the sea stretched out in all directions, a hazy-blue and sparkling plain.

The Collector squinted. There was a tiny, dark spot on the sea—Ar's Adrudian mill, a rebuild of the structure that had burned down on the same rock island sixteen years earlier. The Collector stared at it, fiddling with the brim of his hat, until Caladrius twittered at him from ahead.

"I know. I'm coming," the Collector said, turning to follow her.

He walked parallel to the procession on the street, moving quicker now that he was above the crowd. The rooftops were empty save for the occasional group of Quandary Thieves. The Collector drifted to the side to stay out of their way, holding the Jar of Lights close to his hip. Thieves were the only citizens of Ar to travel over rooftops. They were outlaws, traitors, and revolutionaries, and rooftops were a quick escape from the City Watch.

King Faraday's palace soon appeared, rising like a towering arm of shiny obsidian, crouched against the shadow of Ar's neighboring mountains. Caladrius touched down on a rooftop overlooking the palace square. The Collector joined her, peering at the wide, blank tiles cooking in the noonday sun. An iron gallows stood in the center of the square, with a tall City Watchman and two black-robed prisoners standing on top.

The Collector glanced at Caladrius as she settled on his shoulder.

"So, here it is." He stared at the gallows, flexing his fingers on the Jar of Lights. "And it's *them,* too."

Caladrius chirped, tipping her beak at the prisoners: a tall, pale man and a short, round woman. The Collector's stomach made an uneasy turn. He hadn't believed it before, but the rumors were true. The condemned were Philip and Lillian Just, the last of the Seven Thrones of Benemourne.

The Seven Thrones weren't related by blood, but they all took the surname Just. They were seven rulers from around Benemourne who earned the name when they stepped into power in Ar—the word *Just* being a kind of clothing in which a ruler could fit. Lillian and Philip were a couple, married for years, and the last surviving members of the Seven Thrones. They had ruled peacefully in Ar with five other Justs until Faraday and his army of strange clockwork inventions had forced them into hiding.

The Collector had a hard time convincing himself that Lillian and Philip really *were* here, plucked from wherever they had been hiding and brought to the palace square to die.

On the gallows, the tall City Watchman busied himself binding Lillian and Philip's hands. He had taken off his Watchman's coat and folded it into a square at his feet. His red tie and crisp white shirt were smooth and neat, a fringe of golden hair falling across his forehead.

A hush fell over the crowd gathered at the edges of the square. The Collector felt it, too—a sudden heaviness, as if the air had weight.

"The King's coming," the crowd murmured to each other, watching the massive, black doors of the palace. The doors were partly obscured by the hulking frame of King Faraday's crimson-sailed warship, parked in its usual place outside the palace steps. The airship was a hulking mass of shining iron and metal. A hatch in its base was propped open, enveloping the top half of an engineer leaning into it, tinkering with the ship's insides.

The crowd quieted, standing stone-still as the palace doors creaked open and King Johannes Faraday emerged.

Shadows spilled over the steps, shrouding Johannes in semi-darkness. His body was huge, and seemed to be growing bigger every time the Collector saw him. He had been tall and lanky sixteen years ago, when the Collector had first laid eyes on him running out of the burning Adrudian mill, but now he towered like a mountain—two feet taller than he had been, and likely a foot wider. His boots clanked like metal drums on the steps, making the crowd shrink back.

"Today," Johannes said from the shadows, his wet voice booming across the square, "today you have come here with me to witness the final death of the old ways."

The Collector's eyes strained. Johannes' black suit blended with the obsidian palace, making him difficult to see. He had eschewed traditional ruler's clothes since he'd overthrown the Justs; instead, he wore plain black jackets and trousers, often too small at the elbows and stretched thin across his barrel-broad chest.

"Philip Just and his wife finally stand on these gallows." Johannes lumbered down the steps, coming closer to the edge of light outside the palace's shadow. "Today, they meet death."

With a flourish, Johannes stepped into the harsh sunlight. A ripple went through the crowd. The citizens of Ar were unused to the sight of him. He was like a spider that hid in the dark, rarely venturing outside the palace.

Johannes looked nothing like he had sixteen years ago. He had rebuilt himself after the pistol misfire, not with doctors and prosthetics, but with brass, iron, and whatever secret technology he used to create clockworks. His chest had been stretched to encompass a thumping network of wheels and belts beneath his skin. An Adrudian engine rumbled where his heart used to be, somehow circulating his blood and powering his insides. The torn skin on his face had been patched with intricately carved brass. His top lip was brass, and his teeth had been replaced by bars of sharpened iron. He had given himself an iron nose, too, wide-set and stronger than it once had been.

The memory of the pistol misfire burrowed into the Collector's gut. He couldn't stop himself imagining Johannes sitting up on that slimy dock and crawling, hand-less, through the smoking remnants of the destroyed mill. Pushing bars of metal into places where bones should have been. Stuffing himself with Adrudian where a heart should have been.

The rumbling of Johannes' engine grew louder as he ascended the gallows' staircase. The City Watchman moved Lillian and Philip aside to make way for the King, shuffling to the very edge of the iron lattice. Beads of sweat popped up on his forehead.

"My friends, there are but three Justs left—two of whom will die today," Faraday said, addressing the crowd. He smiled snidely at Lillian and Philip, who met his gaze with level stares. "The one Just remaining is the youngest. Their most recent addition, hardly initiated, and too young to be loyal to the old ways. The one they call *Princess.* In fact, she has come here today to witness Philip and his wife's executions."

Faraday looked back the way he had come, toward the palace doors and his red-sailed warship. The engineer tinkering inside stood up from beneath the hatch in the ship's base. It was a young woman, her arms streaked with grease and a screwdriver held between her teeth. Her skin was dark brown, and she wore her coiled black hair in a round, cloud-like bun.

The Collector peered through the sunlight's glare. He had heard of this woman, the so-called Princess of the Seven Thrones. A reserved, blade-sharp engineer who had been next in line to join Ar's rulers. If the rumors were true, she had earned the name *Just* only days before King Faraday's overthrow.

The King smiled at her, sunshine gleaming off his iron teeth. The engineer snapped the warship's hatch closed and wiped her hands on the front of her long, blue skirts, leaving streaks of Adrudian Milk below the leather tool belt hanging from her waist.

"Young Winn Just intends to leave the Seven Thrones behind where they belong." Faraday's grin widened. He beckoned with his brass hand, and Winn walked around the side of the warship and faced the crowd. "She feels no sorrow for the death of her companions. I trust her."

Winn's expression was unreadable. The corners of her rounded lips pinched. She remained still as if she were frozen, her hand resting at the buckle of her tool belt.

Faraday stepped to the very edge of the gallows. The iron lattice creaked under his weight. "So, my friends, even as I complete my promise to bring ruin to the Seven Thrones, I have decided to break my word in this small way." The tall Watchman flinched as the King opened his arms again, nearly brushing up against him. "I will leave one Just alive. She will be an asset to this kingdom. A great engineer."

Winn stood, stony-faced, as chatter rose from the crowd. King Faraday thumped a hand to his chest and glanced at the Watchman.

"Get on with it, then."

The Watchman placed ropes around Lillian and Philip's necks. His arms were trembling. Near the palace, Winn Just returned to the warship and re-opened the hatch, bending and reaching to toy with the gears and wires within. When Faraday pulled the lever and the trapdoors dropped, she didn't look up, either at her hanging friends or at the King.

THE CROWD DISPERSED AS QUICKLY as it had assembled. Lillian and Philip were cut down and laid across the platform at the King's feet. Seeing them, the Collector pushed his hat down on his head, picked up the Jar of Lights, and drifted down to the square. He walked over the black tile and rose onto the iron-latticed platform, forgoing the stairs. Caladrius kept tight hold of his shoulder as he touched down onto the platform and stood, eyeing the King.

King Faraday looked down at Lillian and Philip's bodies, sunken eyes surveying the folds of their black robes. Beside him, the Watchman donned his coat. With a start, the Collector caught sight of a gold badge winking above his lapel.

"That's no ordinary Watchman," the Collector said to Caladrius, who tipped her head side-to-side. "He's the Head Inspector."

The Head Inspector of Ar was the leader of King Faraday's entire City Watch fleet. The Collector had overheard the rumor that the new Inspector was a young, inexperienced man in his mid-twenties—some wealthy family's son making a change of career. The Head Inspector buttoned his coat, sandy skin gone greenish as if he had swallowed something rotten. His features were angular, sharpened by his frown.

"You're sweating, Cameron," King Faraday said. He rapped his finger on his chin, brass hitting brass with a metallic *tap-tap-tap*.

The Head Inspector, Cameron, paused in the middle of donning his black Watchman's gloves. "Sweating, sir?"

Faraday's eyes rolled from the Justs, to Cameron, and back again. The Collector was reminded of two shifting black coals.

"I will be out of the city tomorrow night," Faraday said.

Cameron lifted his head. "Going to the Adrudian mill again, Your Highness?"

"Yes." Faraday's chest-engine pulsed behind his words, punctuating them with a deep, scraping rumbling.

If the Collector looked close enough, he could see the fabric of Faraday's black waistcoat depressing with each beat. "Some days ago, I was visited by an old friend. He reminded me of business I have there."

"What is the business?"

Faraday's finger *tap-tap-tapped* on his chin. "A service to another friend, from a long time ago."

Cameron tugged on the wrist of his second glove, straightening it. His expression was solemn. "Another ... old friend, sir?"

The tapping on Faraday's chin stopped. He looked up, turning his eyes on Cameron, who froze with his hands poised out in front of him.

"You *are* inquisitive, aren't you?" Faraday said.

Cameron cleared his throat. He clasped his hands, gloves squeaking against each other. "I'm sorry, Your Highness."

The King exhaled, hot air rushing with another turnover of his chest. He reached out his large, brass hand and slid his fingers down Cameron's face.

"What I wouldn't give to have your inquisitive face, Cameron." Faraday's voice was so low it was almost a whisper. "Maybe someday I will."

Cameron's mouth clamped shut. The King's teeth flashed black as he stretched his bottom lip into a smile. Then, without another word, he lowered his hand and clumped down the steps of the platform.

The Head Inspector stood for a moment, letting a long

breath out through barely parted lips. He adjusted his gold pin. Then, with one short, fleeting look at the bodies of the Justs, he strode down the steps and walked toward a line of Watchmen on the street below. His posture was as tense as a metal bar.

The Collector stared after him until Caladrius chirped softly in his ear. She fluttered from his shoulder and settled on the brim of his hat.

"You're right," the Collector replied. He was alone with the Justs now, and thankful he wouldn't have to collect their souls under the shadow of Johannes Faraday. "Let's do it."

He kneeled beside the bodies, sitting the Jar of Lights down at his side. Pushing away his thoughts, the Collector reached out, laid a hand over Philip's chest, and *pulled.* A soft glow bubbled up beneath his fingers. He cupped the soul in his hands and began to guide it toward the Jar of Lights.

But instead of rolling off his hands into the lantern's bulb, the soul suddenly zipped through the Collector's fingers like a thick bubble of smoke. It hovered, glowing, in the air in front of him.

He stared at it. Caladrius twittered, pushing on the brim of his hat so it wobbled up and down.

"Wait," the Collector said, and tried to grasp the soul again. This time it darted out of the path of his fingers and fell in a smooth arc to rest on the chest of the second body, Lillian.

The Collector shook his head. "Cal, what's ...?"

He didn't know how to finish the sentence. Human souls never showed awareness after being collected. The Collector didn't even think of them as *human* anymore—he thought of them as a kind of spectral power, like the power that made Adrudian glow. There had never been a soul that slipped through his fingers, moved about in the air, or sat *looking* at him, as this one did. A chill passed down the Collector's spine, making his skin tense with goosebumps.

Caladrius was confused, too. She made a low noise, and, after a moment's hesitation, fluttered down to perch beside the soul on Lillian's chest. It bobbed in the air, nudging her with its light. She nudged it back, ruffling her wings. The soul brightened and circled her, drawing a delighted twitter from her beak. The Collector sensed an interaction taking place, as if bird and soul shared a silent language. He swallowed the urge to draw Caladrius away.

Finally, Caladrius looked up at him and chirped. The Collector gawked at her.

"I don't understand."

She lowered her head, pointing down at the body beneath her, and chirped again.

"Okay." The Collector raised his hands. "Did it ... *tell* you something?"

Caladrius hopped up to his shoulder and nipped his earlobe, as if to say, *Trust me.*

The Collector nodded. He pressed his hand to

Lillian's chest, careful not to touch Philip's soul, and *pulled.* Another bubble of light bloomed beneath his palm. He tried to lift the soul up as he had done the last, but it slipped through his fingers and joined the other. The two souls circled each other and floated at eye level with the Collector.

"Hello?" he said.

Some part of him feared they would say something in response. But they didn't—they lifted themselves through the air and sailed down the steps of the gallows and onto the street below. The Collector gaped, dumbfounded, as they bobbed over to the Head Inspector, who had made his way down the line of Watchmen. When Cameron left the palace square, disappearing down a side street, the two souls followed him.

Caladrius cooed. The Collector pressed his hand to his chest.

"I don't think that's a good idea."

She cooed again, then opened her wings and leaped into the air, straight after Cameron and the two souls.

Watching her fly away, the Collector had a peculiar feeling, as if he were falling backward off a cliff. Surprise was uncomfortable. Even worse was the creeping curiosity —a feeling that reminded him of a night sixteen years ago, and his hand flush against the side of a boat.

He got to his feet and picked up the Jar of Lights.

Caladrius and the two souls were waiting for him at the mouth of a dark alleyway. Caladrius sang out when she saw the Collector, hopping onto his shoulder and giving his neck an affectionate rub with the top of her head.

"This is definitely not a good idea," he said to her.

Still, when the two souls floated into the alleyway, he pushed his hat low onto his head and followed.

The alleyways of Ar were narrow and dark, with tall buildings on either side slicing the daylight. Pathways in this part of the city didn't follow any map. They were a maze that could be navigated only by those familiar with the dingiest parts of Ar: Quandary Thieves, contract killers, and their ilk.

The souls led the Collector and Caladrius in a zigzag through dim, brick-lined passages until they eventually caught up with Cameron, walking quickly with his hands clasped behind his back. He came to a stop at an inconspicuous, grimy alcove, streaked with slimy drips from round pipes set low into the walls. Looking over his shoulder, Cameron stepped into the semi-darkness.

The Collector drifted to the mouth of the alcove, raising the Jar of Lights. He watched as Cameron pressed his back against the wall and slid down to the ground, pulling his legs up to him.

"Why are we here?" the Collector asked the two souls, whispering even though he knew Cameron couldn't hear. "Where have you brought us?"

The souls hovered in the air next to him, offering no answer. In the silence, the sound of footsteps approached. The Collector turned as a familiar figure appeared out of the darkness, holding up her long skirts. She strode so quickly the Collector didn't have time to move—she walked through him, making his insides feel sticky.

"Cameron Agustin," she said, stepping into the alcove. She kneeled in front of him, her tool belt bunching at her waist.

Cameron lifted his head. "Winn Just."

They hugged, holding on to one another for a long time. The souls of Lillian and Philip bobbed in the air, casting white light on them both.

"You're okay?" Winn ducked her head to meet Cameron's eyes. Her voice was a soft rasp, issuing from the shadows beneath her hair.

Cameron gave a small nod. "It's not me I'm worried about. Your friends—I'm so—" He swallowed, mopping the sweat from his forehead with the back of his sleeve. "I could hardly look at them after."

Winn hung her head so low her chin nearly touched her chest. She took a deep breath and held it, her fingers fiddling with the tools around her waist. "It's how they wanted it. They knew what they were doing."

The two of them stayed silent for a moment, examining the greasy stones beneath their feet. Eventually Winn stood, wiped tears from her face, and reached into her pocket, pulling out a box of matches. She stuck a match between her teeth, chewing on the wooden end like a toothpick. The side of her small, short-bridged nose was smeared with engine grease.

Cameron sniffed and dragged a finger beneath his eyes. "Did you bring the box?"

Winn reached into her pocket again and pulled out something small and cylindrical. The Collector stared at it —a round wooden box layered with shiny discs and knobs of copper.

"Give me a second ..." Winn held the match between her teeth as she started pressing and spinning the box in her hands, pushing buttons and twisting pieces of copper over its surface.

Cameron's eyes widened. "It's a puzzle." He stood and studied her fingers as they moved. "You can solve it?"

"I built it," Winn said around the match.

She pressed her thumb over one last button and held the box up on the palm of her hand. Four long strips of wood emerged out of each side. They bent at the middle and touched down onto Winn's palm like the legs of a spider.

"It clings to machinery," Winn said, "and stays there until I unlock it. I designed this one to catch and echo voices."

Cameron stared at her. "You hid this ...?"

"In the King's heart, yes. In his engine." Winn held it up for Cameron to see. "It's called a Listening Spider. I installed it a week ago, then took it out yesterday.

Lillian and Philip were very specific. With Faraday's guard down, they thought I might be able to catch something."

The box lifted itself up on her hand, its sleek wooden legs stretching.

Cameron palmed the fabric of his tie. "So, you caught something."

Winn nodded. She pressed the top of the box with her finger. A scratchy, muffled sound came out, like the beginnings of a recording on a phonograph. The Collector drew back, but Caladrius tittered, encouraging him to listen.

"*How did ... where have you been?*" The sound was garbled and quiet, but it was unmistakably the voice of Johannes Faraday.

"*Waiting. In the mines.*"

This was another voice, drawing out the word as if savoring its taste. It sounded like a cold wind. Empty, lifeless. Not human at all. The Collector shivered, pulling his arms close to his sides.

"*In my workshop ... and now you're here. Then it must be ...*" Faraday sounded shaken. "*She's awake. I—I should have known. My clockworks have been mining less Adrudian. She's trying to get my attention, isn't she?*"

The second voice crept in through a cloud of static. "*Yes. She is growing impatient. She's given you time enough to enjoy the gift of her power. You must find what you lost and try again to open the door.*"

Their next words were drowned out by the rumbling

of Faraday's engine. Cameron brought his face to the box, trying to make out the sound.

When Faraday's words clarified, he was saying, "… *and what must I do?"*

"Send me," the second voice breathed. *"I will retrieve the lock. Then you must return it to the mines, and to the House of Matchsticks."*

Cameron flinched, as if the phrase struck an unknown chord inside him. The Collector glanced at Caladrius, his lips pressing into a frown. *The House of Matchsticks.* Where had he heard that name?

"How will …" Faraday's voice descended under the static again, unintelligible. "… *the lock?"*

"It is with the girl. In Casret Watch Academy. She doesn't know … the wearer forgets." The second voice paused, elongating its breaths. *"Send me. I will find her and …"*

Its voice quieted beyond what the recording could hear.

"Then go. Bring the lock," Faraday said. His voice faded out and in. "*I will travel to my workshop tonight."*

The sound from the box stretched thin, followed by a series of clicks. Winn pressed the top and the legs whirred and retracted, disappearing into the cylinder.

Cameron swallowed, leaning against the alcove wall. "I don't understand."

"Neither do I." Winn dropped the box back into her toolbelt and rubbed her hands together. "But Lillian and

Philip's suspicions were correct. Faraday's workshop is in those Adrudian mines. It's the only place he could be keeping the secret to his clockwork inventions." She passed the match to the other side of her mouth. "We need to find out what the secret is. I can't rebuild the Seven Thrones without it."

At Winn's mention of them, the souls of Lillian and Philip soared into the alcove and circled her, alighting gently all over, resting in her hair, on her shoulders, at the tip of her nose. The Collector's mouth fell open—they *did* remember. They remembered who they had been, and who had been their friend.

Cameron exhaled slowly. "You mean to sneak into the mines."

"Yes."

"When?"

"How soon will everyone we need be here?"

Cameron curled his top lip between his teeth, thinking. "Not long. I've done everything you've asked. I've spoken with the Quandary of Thieves. They're sending for someone from the southeast—a young man. Jameson. He's supposed to be their best."

Winn pulled at a stray curl springing from her hair bun. "What about the Quandary's spy? At Casret Academy?"

"We've been corresponding. I've sent a friend—Neave, her name is—to break the spy out of the Academy. Hopefully Neave and the spy can get to this *lock* before Faraday's friend finds it." Cameron ran a hand over his neck, scratching at a line of stubble beneath his jaw. "Who was that, do you think? On the recording? The voice ... didn't sound right."

Winn shrugged. "Never heard the voice before. I'd remember if I did."

Cameron patted the pockets of his Watchman's coat. "Whoever it is, they're going to be at the Academy looking for the lock, too. Neave's going to need help." He tugged back his sleeve and squinted at his watch in the darkness. "There's still time to catch the afternoon ferry to the mill."

Winn nodded. "Go, then. Talk to ... what was his name again? Your old Treasurehunting rival."

"Jack."

"Jack. He'll be useful."

Cameron slipped his sleeve back over his wrist. "He's going to be easy to persuade," he said, and for a moment his eyes sparkled. "He's a sore loser."

Winn dropped her match and ground it beneath the heel of her boot as if it were a cigar. "This is beyond the pride of Treasurehunters, Cameron. Hunting for artifacts and keystones is one thing. Taking back Benemourne is another." She paused, then added softly, "I hope Lillian and Philip knew what they were doing, leaving me in charge."

Cameron smiled lightly. "You're the Princess of the Seven Thrones. The first new Just in twenty years."

"It's just a nickname. I got a few days as a Throne, that's it. I was so young."

"Well, now you're old enough to know when to ask for help." Cameron rested a comforting hand on her shoulder. "That's a pretty good start for a Princess."

They left the alcove together, passing through the Collector. The sludgy feeling of their movement made him tense. He waited until their footsteps faded into the muffled sounds of voices and traffic from the main road.

"For what purpose did you bring us here?" the Collector asked, staring at souls of the Justs.

The souls made no answer except for a swaying in the air and a brief brush against his cheekbone. He grimaced. Their touch left a tingling trail on his skin.

"I cannot help you. I cannot get involved."

The souls sailed to the left, huddling under Caladrius' wings. She whistled a song in reply.

"This is not who we are," the Collector said, but he could hear his own voice growing weak. "We don't ... interfere."

Except once, he thought, *a long time ago, when I pushed a boat.*

Faraday had mentioned a lock. Hadn't the Collector seen a mother drop a pendant into a baby bundle? Hadn't there been the glint of a keyhole cutout shining at the end of a bronze chain?

Caladrius chirped and bumped his chin with the top of her head. The Collector looked over at her, heart pounding. If the Collector's fears were true, they had made a difference in humanity—they had changed the events of that night. The shades of such a thing were vast, unknowable, and wrong. He shuddered.

The souls of the Justs flared, as if listening to his thoughts. They made one last, lazy circle in the air, bright against the darkness of the alley like stars against the night sky. Then they fell slowly into the Jar of Lights, where they would stay until they heard the call of another voice from somewhere far beyond.

4

A STRANGER IN THE FOREST

ISALINE

Isaline dragged herself from the examination arena floor and retrieved her bag and overcoat. She had failed her Weapons Portion, but she still had to get ready for her Survival Portion.

Wiping her eyes, she pushed into the changing room and pulled her Survival Portion outfit out of her bag. The all-weather jacket slipped over her new bruises. She tucked her red pendant under her shirt, pressing it close.

Stupid, stupid, stupid. It had been bad judgment to try to disarm the clockwork. She should have just tried to keep her weapon in her hand, like the rest of the students had obviously done. If there were any that said they had disarmed the clockwork this year, they were lying. They *had* to be.

Sniffing, Isaline locked her bag and maroon overcoat in one of the wooden chests lining the wall. She stepped up to the sink and twisted the tap. Cool water flowed over her hands, shocking her overheated skin. She rubbed water over her face and glanced in the mirror. Her lip was split, she had a bruise making its way up her right cheekbone, and there were small cuts all over her skin that were oozing blood. Droplets of water clung to her eyelids, dripping around her brown, glassy eyes. She splashed more water on her face.

"Get it together," she said into her hands.

Out on the sparring floor, the examiners had reappeared and were waiting for her. They stood statue-like, lined up as they had been on the observation deck. The light spilling from the open double doors behind them made it difficult to see their faces, but looking down the line, Isaline noticed that the Headmaster had left.

"Are you ready to proceed?" It was the woman who had conducted her Weapons Portion—the woman Isaline had never met.

Isaline cleared her throat. "Yes."

The woman scrutinized her. She was young for a guest examiner. Isaline guessed a few years older than twenty. This close to the end of the year, Casret had a scarcity of professors willing to adjudicate the final Weeklong Reviews. Guest examiners weren't unusual, but this woman wasn't a stuffy Head Watch-type, judging by her fitted black coat and dark purple boots. She gave Isaline the impression of a sleek-feathered bird with its wings tucked close around its body.

"Can you confirm that you have no supplies or tools on your person?" the woman asked. Her hair was the same pitch-black as her outfit, gathered in a long, tight braid that draped across her right shoulder.

Isaline toed the springy floor. She had a hard time meeting the woman's shrewd eyes. "I have no supplies or tools."

"Can you confirm that you have no food or water on your person?"

"Yes."

"Then let's begin."

The woman bent to pick up a bag sitting on the floor by her boots. As she did, her braid swung away from her body, revealing the twinkle of an orange pin sitting at her lapel.

Isaline's mouth fell open.

A Treasurehunter.

The pin was distinctive: a dead tree, its curling roots spread with dots of gold. Isaline had never seen a Treasurehunter in person. They didn't stray far from Ar, the closest city to the Shute, the ancient forest where they hunted for lost or stolen artifacts. Treasurehunters *definitely* didn't come all the way to Casret Academy to be guest adjudicators for exams.

There was a small, secret smile on the Treasurehunter's face. She cocked her head to the side. "You are aware of the rules of the Survival Portion of the exam?"

Isaline pinched the skin on the back of her hand, half-expecting to wake up in her dormitory, buried beneath her gray coverlet. Nothing happened. The orange pin remained, peeking out from behind the woman's braid.

"I …" Isaline said, dumbstruck. "The—the rules. Don't die, primarily."

The Treasurehunter's smile widened, green eyes glinting from within the shadow of her face. She reached into her bag and produced a small, pistol-shaped object.

"Oh, yes." Isaline's cheeks were burning. "Right. The flare."

"Report back here in a week." The Treasurehunter handed Isaline the small flare gun. Her fingers were smooth, pale, and tipped with black-painted nails. "You are not to have contact with anyone unless the examiners come and get you. If you are in life-threatening distress, activate your emergency flare, and the examiners will arrive at your location shortly. Please be advised that if you activate the flare, the Survival Portion will end, and you will receive failing marks."

Isaline slid the flare into the specially designed loop on the leg of her pants. If there was any rule she was familiar with, it was this one. She had activated the flare on all four of her previous Weeklong Reviews.

"You must be in good health when you return, and your skills will be judged accordingly. Do you have any questions?"

Isaline shook her head, fiddling with the bottom of her jacket. She couldn't help but notice the woman's right hand resting at her side, as if it were used to hovering next to a Treasurehunter's weapons belt. Sun shone in through the space between her arm and her hip, making a misshapen circle of light.

"Because you have failed the Weapons Portion, please be advised that you must pass the Survival Portion of the exam." The Treasurehunter paused, fixing Isaline with an expression she had no idea how to read. "You will fail the entire Weeklong Review if you get disqualified during the Survival Portion. Water, food, a fire, and basic tools are a must for a passing grade."

Isaline had prepared herself to hear this, but her heart still plummeted. She wasn't a survivalist like Nalissa had trained to be, and she wasn't naturally good at things she hadn't trained for. Sometimes she wasn't even good at the things she *had* trained for.

The Treasurehunter frowned, studying Isaline, waiting for a response. Isaline looked at the other examiners. Their faces were cold, closed.

"Can I ... go now?" she asked weakly.

The Treasurehunter's eyes twinkled. "If you're ready, then the Survival Portion has begun. You may exit out of the Training Center and into the forest. Explore all you like, but stay within the bounds of the section for final year students."

Isaline looked past the examiners and through the open double doors. All she had to do was get through those doors and this whole nightmare conversation would be over. She would never be comfortable in the forest—and she was sure to get lost, as the layout of the final year section was kept secret—but at least she would be alone.

Taking a deep breath, Isaline walked forward. The line of examiners parted to let her through, quiet as a graveyard. The Treasurehunter's sharp eyes followed her all the way to the door.

"By the way ..."

Isaline looked over her shoulder. The Treasurehunter paused, one long hand still resting at her hip. Her face was indecipherable.

"Good luck," she said.

Half an hour later, Isaline trudged through the forest, muttering to herself. The air was starting to heat up as morning edged toward afternoon. Sunshine speckled the ground, sliding this way and that as the canopies of trees swayed in the breeze.

She was heading north, toward where she hoped there might be water. Her body twinged with each step, but she pushed herself to keep walking. The more space she put between herself and the Academy, the better. She'd lived at Casret for five years—she'd never lived anywhere else—but it was the last place she wanted to be right now.

A tangle of low-hanging branches blocked the path

ahead of her. Isaline turned right and plunged deeper into the woods, stepping over scrubby plants and dodging the gnarled roots of trees. The Weeklong Review was the only time of year she spent more than a day away from her dorm room. Leaving the school left her disoriented, the same feeling she'd had when she first arrived at the Academy from the orphanage in Fort Upper, eleven years old and terrified.

Nalissa had already been living at the Academy for a few days before Isaline arrived. She was there when the Headmaster led Isaline into the dormitory, waiting at the other side of the room with her hands wound into a ball. Isaline had been instantly suspicious of Nalissa. There hadn't been anyone like her at the orphanage. Her confidence lit her like a spotlight.

When Isaline couldn't find the words to introduce herself, Nalissa smiled and took her hand. She'd pulled Isaline out of their room, down the stairs, and into a hidden alcove between shrubs at the base of the dormitory where no one could hear them. The cold stone of the dormitory building pressed into their backs, their legs disappearing shin-deep in a snarl of shiny leaves.

"We're going to be best friends," Nalissa had whispered to her.

Like so many nights in the years following, Isaline had listened while Nalissa talked. She learned that Nalissa was placeless too, and had been discovered on the streets of Fort Upper. Isaline was shocked that someone like

Nalissa had come from nowhere; she seemed to belong everywhere at once.

When Nalissa's secrets had run out, she and Isaline had climbed the stairs of the dormitory again, bypassing their room and sneaking onto the roof. Isaline had gripped Nalissa's hand and peered down the side of the building, dizzy with the height and how small everything looked on the ground below. She felt as if she would topple over the edge just by looking. Her arms stiffened and she backed away from the drop, releasing Nalissa's hand and sitting hard in the middle of the roof.

Nalissa had stayed at the edge, fanning her arms out. She beckoned to Isaline, but Isaline shook her head, gazing as Nalissa danced and tiptoed like she'd been balancing on rooftops her entire life.

"Turn upside down," Nalissa had said, leaning to the side as if she were going to cartwheel. "Gives you a new perspective."

A loud rumble above the forest yanked Isaline out of her thoughts. She stopped, one hand resting against the bark of the nearest tree, and looked up. The long iron struts of a train bridge peeked through the canopy of leaves—one of the many bridges that crisscrossed high above Casret Academy's training area. The bridges led out from the train station in Fort Upper, carrying passengers to cities and villages throughout Benemourne.

Isaline's stomach twisted. After the Weeklong, there would be no Nalissas out in the world to take her hand

and lead her. Unlike Nalissa, no future had solidified for Isaline; if she failed, she would never be a City Watch, or have the chance—no matter how small—to take a train to Ar. She would be nothing, just a girl with nowhere to go.

The train's whistle sang out, followed by the rhythmic chugging of wheels. Isaline gazed at the wheels barreling across the bridge. Hot, Adrudian-scented air wafted down into her face. She stood and listened until the noise faded into the distance. Then she let out a long breath, squeezed her hands together, and strode toward the thickest part of the forest.

After walking for long minutes, Isaline sidestepped through a thick line of trees and found herself in a large, round clearing.

A towering, twist-rooted oak tree sat at the southeastern end of the clearing, its branches reaching high above the surrounding canopies. Its emerald leaves rustled in the warm breeze, harmonizing with the twitters of birds as they darted around the branches. There were too many birds to count, but Isaline could tell they were starlings—black-feathered with shiny patches that gleamed blue and purple in the light.

The forest floor in the clearing was smooth, green grass. Isaline picked her way toward a comfortable-looking spot between two of the tree's spreading roots. Her muscles were aching—she needed to find water, but her body screamed for rest.

As she lowered herself to the grass, a branch cracked outside the clearing.

Isaline's head shot up. Were the examiners watching? They left the students alone during the Survival Portion, but she wouldn't put it past that sharp-eyed Shute Treasurehunter to follow her out here.

The trees around the clearing were closely packed together, branches knitting like a zipper. Goosebumps rose along Isaline's arms. Why did she get the feeling she was being watched?

"Hello?" She got to her feet, wincing as her calf muscles smarted. "Who's there?"

There was no response. Isaline leaned down and picked a fallen branch off the ground at her feet.

"I know you're there." She advanced toward the tree line, branch held out. Her heart sped to a gallop in her chest. A vision of Marik Taylor's monster materialized in her mind's eye: human-like, but slithering along the ground like a snake, arms stretched out in front of its body.

He'd said something else, too—something that echoed in her mind as if he were sitting next to her, staring at Nalissa over her shoulder.

There was something wrong with the eyes.

Another branch cracked. It came from the tangle of leaves right in front of her.

Isaline cried out in surprise. She thrust the stick she

was holding through the mass of branches and leaves, as if to stab whatever was hiding. The branch didn't hit anything, but something small and dark suddenly rushed from the base of the trees, over the ground and toward her feet.

She lurched backward, shouting. The branch flew out of her hand. Her ankle hit a rock and she stumbled, falling on her backside. Pain from her bruised tailbone shot through her spine. The thing that had sped out of the trees ran across the clearing, a brown-tinged blur, and plunged through the tree line. She got a good look before it disappeared.

A squirrel. It was a squirrel.

Isaline huffed and smacked the grass with her hands. *No, no, no.* She would never pass the Survival Portion if she was going to act like a first-year Watchling, afraid of her own shadow.

Rubbing her shoulders, Isaline rocked to her feet and started back toward the oak tree. She got halfway there before another sound froze her in place. It came floating across the clearing—not a cracking branch this time, but something higher and longer. Isaline cocked her head to the side, listening.

It's laughing. She whirled, her shoulders coming up around her ears. *Someone's laughing.*

A figure stepped out from behind a tree.

"Really," it said, "that was some attack."

Isaline stared slack-jawed at the new arrival. She had

expected to see Marik Taylor's monster, groaning and leering at her with a set of malformed eyes. This wasn't a monster, though—it was a boy about her age, maybe a little older, wearing a deep green overcoat. His deep brown hair sat in a tousled pile on top of his head.

"Who—*the hell*—are you?" Isaline said. Her chest started to heave, throat closing tight. She spun around looking for another fallen branch, but there weren't any near enough to grab.

The boy raised his hands in a gesture of peace. His fingers were long and studded with sparkling rings.

"Hey, now," he said. "I got here first. I happen to be the person whose clearing you're in."

Isaline gawked at him. His black, pointed boots were dulled by layers of dirt and dust. Leaves poked out of the fabric of his coat, and he had a twig stuck through his top buttonhole, stark against his pinkish complexion. If it weren't for the rings, he would have looked like a forest sprite, sprung into existence from the bark of a tree.

"How long have you been there?" Isaline demanded. "Were you just standing there watching me? Were you *following* me?"

The boy snorted. His jawline was shadowed with the beginnings of dark facial hair, evidence of a few days of travel. "Please," he said. "Once again, *you* are in *my* clearing." He pointed toward the oak tree. "Look."

Isaline followed his gaze. Sure enough, there was a pile

of chopped firewood that had been stacked next to the oak tree's trunk. The pile was hidden, though not so hidden that she shouldn't have seen it. Her shoulders slumped. She really was terrible at Country Watch training.

The boy ran a hand through his hair, sending a leaf or two spiraling to the ground. His chin and nose were pointed, marten-like. "Listen," he said, "I realize you're from the school and you're probably on one of those test things—"

"Weeklong Reviews," Isaline said reflexively.

He clapped his hands together. "Right. If you stay out of my way, we won't need to see each other. I'm just passing through."

Isaline clenched her fists. He was taller than her, but she locked her knees and raised her shoulders, assuming a City Watch posture. "You're not supposed to be here, you know. How did you even get *in* here?"

The boy shrugged. He didn't seem to be all that intimidated by her, or even interested. "Just walked in." He gestured behind him. "There was an empty guardhouse west of here. You all lose some guards, or ...?"

They *had* lost some guards—the same ones she and Nalissa had talked about last night. Isaline's voice locked in her throat.

"Look." The boy smiled and took a step forward. Isaline took a step back, shuffling against the roots of the oak tree. He raised his palms again. "I really am just passing through. I've come from Sunrest. I'm headed north to take a train to Lower Village, and then to Ar."

Isaline flicked her eyes northward. The train station was north of the clearing, if she had her bearings.

"You're from Sunrest, going to Ar." She had studied her map of Benemourne close enough to know the geography surrounding Ar better than her own fingerprint. "Seems like you're taking a pretty long detour."

He dug the toe of his boot into the grass. "Passenger ships from Sunrest to Ar are rare. Better to travel north first."

"And take a train to Lower Village?" she asked, skeptical.

"Would you rather go through the Shute?"

He had her there. The Shute lay between Sunrest and Ar, and traveling through it was a last resort. Only Treasurehunters went into that forest, and even they came back in smaller numbers.

The boy reached into his pocket and pulled out a torn envelope. "Here." He held it out to her, palm up so she could see the silver and gold bands of his rings. "This is my summons, if you want proof."

Isaline looked from his face to the envelope, and back again. Something in his expression told her he was telling the truth. The way he was standing—relaxed, shoulders loose—didn't indicate a Watch, and it was clear from his appearance that he'd been traveling for a few days. She marched forward, grabbed the envelope from his outstretched hand, and returned to the other side of the clearing.

The letter slid easily out of the envelope. It was printed on thick, cream-colored paper. Official.

Jameson, the first line read.

You have been summoned to Ar on official Quandary business. Please arrive in the city at two weeks past the turn of the month. Upon arrival at Quandary Headquarters, check in and an agent will take you to your employer.

Isaline exhaled through her teeth. *Thieves' Quandary.*

She had been taught about the Quandary in her classes. They were soulless outlaws targeting the King's supporters. Isaline peered over the top of the letter at the boy, who stood quietly with his hands in his pockets, studying the branches of the oak tree. She narrowed her eyes. The sparkling rings made sense. What wealthy family had he stolen them from?

She folded the letter back up. He glanced down at her.

"So, you're just traveling through." She put on the best City Watch voice she could, hoping against hope that her words wouldn't lock up and disappear again. "You're still trespassing on Casret property. On Thieves' Quandary business, no less. Give me one reason not to pull the trigger on my flare right now."

He let out an abrupt laugh, which flickered and died when he saw her expression. "Oh, you're serious."

Isaline glowered at him, pressing her fingers into the envelope so hard it creased.

"I mean ..." The boy shrugged again, rubbing the back of his neck. "I'm pretty sure that would cut your exam short, wouldn't it?"

Isaline relaxed her hold on the envelope. He was right. If she pulled the flare, she might be disqualified by default, and she couldn't afford to be disqualified. She prayed none of the examiners were spying.

She held the letter back to him. He smiled again, eyes crinkling into pleasant half-moons.

"You're Jameson?" Isaline asked him.

"Jame." He stuck out his hand. "What's your name?"

She ignored both his hand and his question. "If you haven't noticed, Jame, I have some injuries I need to attend to—"

He flashed another grin. "I've seen worse."

"—and I have to find water and start a fire." Isaline glanced up at the sky. It was still afternoon, but it would be dark soon enough, and someone needed to keep an eye on him. "I'm going to need to hang out here, if you, *the owner* of this clearing, are okay with that."

Jame shrugged off his overcoat and turned to drape it over a nearby branch. He was tall and agile-looking—a Thief's stature. She looked away when he glanced toward her.

"Permission granted. There's a stream not far from here, by the way." He smoothed the ends of his overcoat so they lay flat. "I'll be here another few days before my train leaves for Lower Village." He paused. "Are you ... surviving, basically?"

"Basically." Isaline sat on one of the oak tree's roots and covered her face with her hands. Her head was throbbing.

Jame reached into the pocket of his overcoat. To Isaline's surprise, he pulled out two long knitting needles and a ball of pear-colored yarn. He sat with his back against a tree. "I won't bother you. I won't even talk," he said. Then, looking up at her, he added, "Unless you want to have a conversation, or whatever."

Isaline arched her eyebrows at him. "I'm not supposed to see or talk to anyone. Especially someone like you."

"Say no more."

He cast his yarn on a needle, passed a glittering hand through his hair, and started to knit.

5

THE WAGER

JACK

Jack had a hunch. He hadn't been sure before, but now he was almost certain less Adrudian ore was coming up from the mines.

He winced as a hot blast of steam curled up and under the sleeve of his heavy heatproof coat. Straightening, he passed the shovel to his other hand. His forearms were going to be soaked and blistered by the end of the day, and his heatproof pants weren't offering him much protection, either. He bent and ran a hand over his calf. Wet inside, of course—his ankles had grown skinny over the past month.

Jack gripped the shovel and pushed it hard into the pile of glowing Adrudian rocks heaped by his foot. Metal scraped against metal as the shovel's tip glanced off the bottom of the tray. He made note of the scrape. Before this week, his shovel had never hit the bottom of the tray. The ore was steaming more, too. It clouded Jack's supposedly fog-free goggles. He swiped the back of his sleeve over his eyes, smearing droplets on the glass.

Rocks of Adrudian ore needed to be activated with heat before they could be shipped out of the mill and used for fuel. Jack had been assigned the job of moving the cooked Adrudian over the tray that connected its cooking vat and its shipping container. Doing so required balancing on the lips of both slick metal containers and passing the ore between them with a shovel. The least Rhody Charlotte could do was give him working goggles. Not that she cared, and not that bad luck got him the job of shoveling cooked Adrudian, either.

"No risk to you or me," Rhody had said to him. "The vat gets too hot, we run the chance of having Milk in there. You know what happens if one of my workers falls in. I lose them to the streets, or worse."

Jack had said nothing. He waited for her to say it. He *wanted* her to say it.

Rhody hacked one of her perpetual coughs into a streaky fist.

"If *you* fall into the Milk," she'd said, "you stay your pretty self, don't you, Blueveins?"

Jack heaved the shovel again, swinging a pile of hot ore over the gap between the containers. His feet were planted so he stood astride the gap, balancing high above the ten feet of space between the edge of the containers and the floor of the mill. Countless times, he had looked down and imagined himself stumbling, slipping through the space between the huge metal vats. In his mind's eye, he never hit the floor of the mill but went through it like a ghost, plunging into the Adrudian mines below. When he hit bottom, no one would look for him. No one would find him. Not unless there was a clockwork down there with eyes.

The turnover machine rolled another heap of ore toward the tray. Holding his breath, Jack passed the shovel over the gap. The shovel was heavier than the Adrudian itself. Porous and hard to the touch, Adrudian was one of the lightest rocks in existence—a fact for which Jack supposed he should be grateful.

As he was digging the shovel into the fresh pile of ore, a muffled voice came from behind him. It rose above the din, but he couldn't tell what it was saying. He dug an earplug out of his left ear.

"Jack." It was Rhody Charlotte's voice. He twisted around and saw her standing on the metal platform skirting the back edge of the shipping container, twirling a pair of goggles by their elastic strap. He could just make out her grimy yellow hair and almost-as-yellow teeth through the fogged-up glass of his goggles. Her odd, red-eyed rat was perched on her shoulder, teeth gnashing on her hair.

"What?" He held his earplug poised a few inches from his head.

"Someone's here to see you. Says it's been a while, and he's got news."

Jack barked a laugh. He pushed the earplug back into his ear. "Tell him I'm busy."

Rhody walked around the edge of the platform and flicked the switch on the panel that controlled the clockwork mechanism on the turnover machine. The machine ground to a screeching halt, rocks of ore clattering down its massive iron scoops.

Jack grunted. He tossed the shovel onto the tray. Rhody leaned on the railing of the platform, giving him a look of sheer ice.

"He twist your arm or something?" Jack said to her, taking out both earplugs and lifting his goggles from his eyes. The interior of the mill came into focus, all dark iron, bursts of orange ore, and people in leather aprons crawling about like ants.

Rhody Charlotte spat, narrowly missing the control panel.

"Doesn't have to," she said. "Head Inspector's got privileges."

Jack followed Rhody on a winding path through the bustling mill toward her office. Bins of gray rags encrusted with Milk lined the aisles, dotted with the shadows of crates being hoisted on pulleys above. He kept his eyes forward, trying to ignore the stares of other mill workers. It had been weeks since he'd returned to work, and still they hadn't grown used to the sight of him. More than one worker stopped what they were doing, wrenched their goggles from their dirt-smeared cheeks, and murmured to the others at their sides.

Adrudian Drinker, Jack imagined them saying.

Rhody rounded a corner, taking them down one of the mill's busiest aisles. Jack stepped to the side as a clockwork lumbered blindly past, pushing a cartful of glowing Adrudian. Its leaden footsteps shook Jack's brain in his skull. He hated working with clockworks. There was something unsettling about being sensed by a machine that shouldn't have senses. King Faraday guarded the mystery of their design from engineers, wanting people to think of his inventions as *alive*, but to Jack, there was nothing lifelike about clockworks. Their movements were the automatic twitch of a dead thing's nerves.

Jack and Rhody circled a line of spindly sorting machines, leaving the busy aisle behind. A jagged, narrow staircase jutting out of the wall came into view. The warden's office was high up on the third story of the mill, its window shining out of the north wall like one huge, yellow eye. Rhody stopped.

"He's up there," she said, pointing.

Jack paused, one foot on the first step. "You're not coming?"

Rhody snapped the elastic on the goggles. "I don't

tangle with the Watch. Especially not Head Watch." She turned and shuffled back the way they had come, the rat on her shoulder eyeing Jack. "Don't take long, Blueveins."

Jack watched her disappear into the throng of workers and machines. For a moment he considered turning around and going back to shoveling ore, but Rhody would come after him again eventually. Besides, Jack knew better than anyone that once Cameron had an idea in his head, he wouldn't leave until he got what he wanted.

Jack sighed and started up the stairs.

It had been months since he'd last seen Cameron. A long time, considering there were years when Cameron hadn't left Jack alone, despite the fact Jack tried to avoid him. He was uncomfortably aware of the overgrown length of his hair. The greasy black strands were sure to be dusted with soot—and when was the last time he'd brushed it? He couldn't remember.

As he climbed the stairs, he caught a glimpse of Cameron through Rhody's office window. The Head Inspector had helped himself to the chair behind the warden's cluttered desk, legs crossed, spinning his substantial ring of keys on a long index finger. His pristine, golden hair, black Watchman's suit, and crimson tie made him look like the red-breasted geese that nested around the mill's island and would harass Jack when he left at the end of the day, honking at him all the way to the ferry.

Steeling himself, Jack pushed the door open. Cameron grinned up at him.

"I didn't think she'd be able to pull you away," he said.

Jack nudged a stack of papers from a chair beside the desk. "You don't wear that gold badge for nothing," he said. Cameron's eyes flicked down to his chest, catching the light reflecting off the badge. "She's scared of you."

Cameron covered the badge with his hand, grimacing. Jack sat in the now-empty chair and crossed his arms.

"So? What do you want?" he asked.

Cameron looked him up and down. "You look like you haven't slept."

"You look like you have."

Another grimace. Jack suppressed a smile, even if it wasn't true; Cameron looked far from well-rested. Bags darkened his eyes, and a line of stubble ran along his jaw—a patch he must have missed with his expensive Watchman's razor this morning. Jack watched as Cameron clasped his hands around his keyring, crisp black gloves folding around a large, gold key that stood out from the rest.

"Lillian and Philip Just were executed four hours ago," Cameron said.

The room tilted. Jack rested his hand on the desk, smearing soot on one of Rhody Charlotte's papers. "They were caught?"

"No. They surrendered."

The words were heavy as boulders. Noise from the mill's engines reverberated through the room, vibrating the floorboards like an earthquake stretched thin. Jack hardly noticed his boots shaking.

"W-when?" was all he could say.

"Two weeks ago." Cameron opened his hands on his knees, fingers uncurling. "They just walked into the palace. There was no trial."

Jack picked up the shabby nub of a pencil and cracked it in half over his thumb. Years ago, Lillian and Philip had been kind to him. When his parents had boarded a ship north and never came back, Lillian had let Jack sleep in their library, a sanctuary filled with books on Benemournian history, the written mythologies of ancient gods, and documents detailing lost ritual sites. The collection had been small, but enough to help Jack study his first maps and draw lines to his first finds.

Even then, Jack knew Treasurehunting was a career reserved for the wealthy. People like Cameron, who inherited giant libraries and mounds of expensive equipment. But Lillian and Philip had inadvertently given him a chance. He'd found himself locked into rivalries with particular Treasurehunters, men with tailored cloaks and white-toothed grins and golden hair. Every time he had come up against Cameron, Jack had been secretly pleased. Not because the sight of Cameron's smug face did Jack any good, but because Jack had measured up with only his skill and the library of Lillian and Philip Just.

He let the halves of the pencil he'd broken fall to the floor. "They lost hope."

"Quite the contrary." Cameron met Jack's eyes, something inscrutable gleaming behind his tiredness. "They made a wager."

"That's not possible," Jack said, leaning further back in his chair. "Certain death is no wager."

Cameron simply looked at him. The corners of his mouth tugged upward, the celebrity smile he used to give Jack before sneaking an artifact from under his nose. That smile had enchanted dozens of people in their circle—men and women and everyone in-between and beyond—and irritated Jack to distraction.

Looking at it now, Jack's stomach tossed. "What could the Justs possibly have on the King? Lillian and Philip were in hiding for years."

Brushing at the thighs of his trousers, Cameron pocketed his keys and stood up. He was so tall in the tiny office that the top of his head bumped the Adrudian lantern hanging from the ceiling.

"Let's go for a walk," he said. "Too many ears here."

Jack slid open the heavy front door of the mill and he and Cameron walked into the cool sea air. The eyes of the other workers had followed them all the way through the building. The sight of the Adrudian Drinker walking out with the Head Inspector would keep them gossiping for weeks. Worse, as they came down from the office, Jack had seen Rhody Charlotte glaring at him from behind a metal cart, promising to make his life hell for being so long away from the shovel. Even her black rat had slunk down her arm and stalked them until they left.

Cameron strolled to the concrete retaining wall lining the rocky shoreline of the island, his black coat waving in the breeze. Jack slid the metal door closed and followed, shivering. The moisture on the insides of his sleeves and pants cooled in the outside air.

"Winn Just is alive," Cameron said, casting around to make sure they were alone. The shoreline was deserted, but still he spoke in a hushed tone.

"So? She won't be for long." Jack crossed his arms, leaning backward against the retaining wall. He had never met Winn, and didn't care to. With Faraday in power, the Seven Thrones and their Princess would fade until they were nothing but names in history books.

"Faraday won't kill her. He sees her as an asset." Despite his exhaustion, Cameron's eyes managed to glint again. "She sees things the other way around."

"And this has something to do with me?"

Cameron nodded. He ran the tip of his index finger over the retaining wall, then examined the smear of dirt left on his gloves, frowning. "Lillian and Philip believed that Faraday's secret workshop was here, on the island. That the King is keeping the plans for his clockworks *down there.*"

He took the dirt-smudged index finger of his glove and pointed it at the ground.

In the mines, Jack thought.

"Winn wants to rebuild the Seven Thrones," Cameron said, "but Faraday can't be killed the way he is. His body is built like one of his clockworks. No one knows how it works or how to stop it, but Lillian and Philip had a hunch that answers could be found here, in the mines."

Jack dug a finger beneath the elastic strap of his goggles, loosening their tight squeeze around his forehead. He had heard engineers whispering about the King's fabled workshop: the spot where Faraday would have built the clockwork army he used to take over Ar's palace. Jack had reckoned the workshop had been destroyed and the blueprints for clockworks along with it.

"It's a hunch," Jack said, giving Cameron a heavy look. "You understand the meaning of a hunch. It's nothing."

"It's something. Lillian and Philip died for it—for Winn's chance to get close to the King. For her chance to study the way he works, and then to find the secret to killing him, down in those mines." Cameron drew up taller. Jack had to raise his head to look at him, squinting against the bright sky. "I'm going with her."

"You can't be serious."

"I am."

"A year ago, maybe. You're not a Treasurehunter anymore. Going into the mines is suicide, you know that."

Cameron rubbed the heel of his hand against his chest, returning Jack's pointed gaze. "Not with Winn, it's not."

"Please," Jack said. "If the clockworks don't rip you apart before you get to the mine shaft, you'll die down there in the dark." He imagined it: yawning tunnels, unmapped corridors, countless caverns filled with emptiness and the stale breath of the deep earth. "Clockwork pickaxers don't need light. There hasn't been light down there since—"

"Since the fire."

"Right." Jack rubbed a hand over his eyes. "Every human pickaxer died down there. They just never came back."

Now there's only machines. Machines and the ghosts of the dead.

"There's more." Cameron stared out over the water. His eyes reflected its sparkling surface, two molten copper coins. "Winn recorded one of Faraday's conversations. The King said Adrudian is being mined less. Not coming up." He looked at Jack askance. "Have you noticed?"

Jack locked his jaw shut, but Cameron knew him well enough to see the answer written on his face. He sighed and dug into the breast pocket of his coat, retrieving his beat-up, spiral bound notebook. He flipped to the center of the notebook and held it out for Cameron to see.

"Less Adrudian today than yesterday, and less Adrudian yesterday than the day before that." Jack flipped through the pages, showing Cameron his hastily scratched notes. "More steam, too. Can't see anything through my goggles, and my arms are burned raw. A shortage is coming up fast. You can already see Ar's lights dimming. I think—" Jack stopped, looking up to see Cameron's thoughtful expression. He drew away, pulling the notebook back. "What?"

"I didn't think you still did this." Cameron inclined his head toward the notebook. "Research."

Jack shoved the notebook back in his pocket, shaking his head. "It's not research. It's nothing."

"Looks like something."

"It's not." Jack turned and propped his elbows on the retaining wall. He stared at the rocks on the other side, avoiding Cameron's eyes. "Let Winn go down into the mines alone. Lillian and Philip spent years hiding, hoping Faraday had a weakness. That he could be killed. Winn Just will die making the same mistake—don't risk your own life."

"Come on, Jack. I won't believe you're not curious," Cameron said. "It's a mystery how he stays alive. How his clockworks operate. You have to wonder."

Jack shook his head, the ends of his hair swishing against the collar of his threadbare coat. "I'm not a Treasurehunter anymore, either."

"Did all those books leak out of your brain, then?" Cameron propped an elbow on the retaining wall, giving Jack a rueful smile. "You know that no one recorded the history of these mines. You know there could be something down there. I know you know—because I know."

Even squinting into the sun, Jack managed to narrow his eyes. "What could you possibly mean by that?"

"*You* read everything *I* read. We used to always end up after the same artifacts, didn't we? I was starting to think you were following me and my team." Cameron winked, one of his copper coin eyes closing. "Now I just assume you're stealing my books, and that includes my book on mining history. Or lack thereof."

Jack scowled. He *had* read the only book he could find on mining history, and Cameron was right—there was almost nothing known about how Adrudian came to be Benemourne's fuel, or how the mines were dug at the bottom of the sea. But he wasn't going to dignify anything Cameron said by agreeing, especially when Cameron had been the one following *him*.

"Of course I know about the mines," Jack said after a moment. "I cook Adrudian ore myself. And I intend to live to cook more." He ran his tongue over his teeth and pushed away from the retaining wall. "This is wasting my time, Inspector. Have a nice ferry ride home."

"Jack."

Ignoring him, Jack cleared his throat and walked toward the mill, balling his hands into fists.

"Jack."

He heaved the door to the mill open. A group of mill

workers dispersed abruptly, pretending they hadn't been gawking, faces pressed to the dirty windows. Jack made to step inside, glowering at them, and Cameron called out again.

"He mentioned the House of Matchsticks."

Jack stopped.

He turned, slowly, on the spot. Cameron leaned on the retaining wall, backlit by the setting sun, his hair flying around his face in the wind.

"What did you just say?" Jack asked.

"You know what I said. He mentioned it on the recording. I heard it myself."

Jack's body went cold. *The House of Matchsticks*. No need to be secretive, saying those words—the phrase would mean nothing to the mill workers retreating into the mill. But to Jack ...

He hadn't thought Cameron would ever say those words to him again. Jack himself had tried to not even *think* them, but of course his mind hadn't obeyed. His thoughts had the habit of turning in circles, running like an Adrudian engine for days without his permission.

"You know what that means, right?" Cameron took two steps forward, boots tapping on the concrete. "The ritual site—"

Jack let the name out of his mouth, heavy and metallic. "The House of Matchsticks."

"Yes, well. According to *your* translation." Cameron waved a hand, the beginnings of a smirk touching his face.

"Whatever you want to call it, I'm ... it could be in the mines."

The statement floated into Jack's ears and snagged. It didn't make sense. He had spent days poring over the handwritten journals of ancients, weeks deciphering the crumbling scrolls of early maps. It had felt *right*, that morning a year ago when he had finally stepped a compass' needles twice over a map to an unexplored part of the Shute. The forest was bursting with hidden treasures, deposits of precious gemstones, and the forgotten sites of ancient rituals. The House of Matchsticks was said to be all three, a cave filled with lost knowledge. A Treasurehunter's dream.

But the map led inside the Shute. Not underground.

"It can't be here," Jack murmured.

Cameron grinned, knowing Jack was caught. He took another two steps closer. "My idea isn't a hunch. It's an opportunity. An opportunity to continue what you and I started. Separately, of course, but I'm here to propose we combine our efforts."

Our efforts. As if Jack hadn't been two steps ahead of Cameron the whole time. As if Jack hadn't been the first to discover the words for *House of Matchsticks* buried in hidden texts. The map had been *his*—Cameron had simply crashed Jack's expedition. Invited himself along.

Saved Jack's life. Maybe.

Jack closed his eyes and counted to five. When he opened them again, he was standing at the head of a crowd of mill workers who were pretending not to stare. He could go inside and try to force himself to think about shoveling ore—but Jack knew he couldn't forget this conversation. Not now that Cameron had stoked an old fire, a burning fixation that licked at his ribs.

Jack slid the door closed on the mill workers, letting out a wheeze.

"Don't lie to me," he said to Cameron, whipping around.

"It's not a lie."

"Sure sounds like one."

"Would it help if I swore on something I love?"

"Besides yourself?"

Cameron snorted. "Next question."

Jack studied the ground, rummaging in his memory. The Shute and the Adrudian mill were a length of water away from each other, far enough to be at opposite edges of the same map. The mill didn't even appear on Jack's hand-drawn map, the constellation of clues that should have led him to the House of Matchsticks.

He opened and closed his hands, wishing he had the map with him. It was hidden in his tiny room in a boarding house in Lower Village, tucked between his lumpy bed and the wall. He had been too afraid to look at the map after the failed expedition, but he couldn't bring himself to throw it out. As time wore on, he started spending long nights staring at it, mind working itself into exhaustion, trying to figure out where they had gone wrong.

"Every document I read pointed to the Shute," Jack said. He never misread documents, not even when he pored over them until his vision blurred. "The Shute is full of old ritual sites. The mines are ... nothing. Bare."

Cameron made a shushing sound, urging him to be quiet. He waved him closer. Jack shuffled forward a few steps.

"We don't know there's nothing down there," Cameron said when they were out of earshot of the mill. He tipped his chin, lips parting to show a row of perfect teeth. "Who's to know? And, Jack, let's not avoid the truth." He shrugged one shoulder, grin fading slightly. "We didn't find the House of Matchsticks in the Shute."

Jack bit his fingernails into his palms. He couldn't argue with that. They had run into each other early in the expedition, Cameron shadowing Jack through the forest as he followed his map. They had argued, then continued together, and then ... what? The memory stopped there, disappeared as if someone had snipped the rest of the expedition off with scissors. An ache settled into Jack's body every time he tried to dig up what he had forgotten.

A sickness made us forget, Cameron had said afterwards. *Or an enchantment.*

Jack didn't believe in enchantments.

"Something happened to us on that expedition." Jack had said this to Cameron before, but his mouth wouldn't stop saying it, as if he could make it true simply by repeating it. "Something tried to kill us. Something took our memory. We didn't find the House of Matchsticks—" A fair assumption, considering he and Cameron had blinked into consciousness hours later at the outskirts of the Shute, half-dead and without any treasure. "But we found a clue. The House of Matchsticks is ... it's just harder to find than I thought. If I could find out what the clue was ..."

"Some clue," Cameron said gravely, pressing his fingers into the scar on his chest, where something in the forest had raked his skin, bloodying them both as they'd escaped. "But it doesn't matter. The expedition failed. You didn't find anything, did you, when you went back to the forest? When you followed your map again?"

Jack pressed his lips together, then said, "No."

"Precisely."

"Did you?"

Cameron shook his head. "I never went back. I've got other things to live for." He examined the tips of his gloves, then looked through his lashes at Jack, eyeing the sides of his face. "Unlike you, apparently."

Jack rubbed a hand over his jaw. His scratchy black beard hid only half of the blue veins etched into his cheeks. "What are you saying?"

"I'm saying it's only a matter of time before the Milk kills you." Cameron's voice had grown quiet. "I'm saying that's why I'm here. You won't find the House of Matchsticks by Drinking Adrudian, Jack."

Jack's eyes twitched. He ran his fingertip beneath his

bottom lids. The exhaustion of countless sleepless nights spent staring at his map had been unbearable, but the pain of the severed memory had been worse. A part of Jack had been ripped away, and whatever had taken it had left something in its place: an intolerable longing, a *pull* in his ribs that he couldn't understand or explain.

He suspected Cameron felt the *pull* too, so he didn't know how Cameron could blame him. Drinking Adrudian had happened hazily, Jack's hands moving of their own accord, tipping his bedside lantern upside down into a cup. Drinking Adrudian Milk was supposed to open the Drinker's head up like a puzzle box, revealing lost memories, visions of the future, the strange workings of the mind.

But it hadn't worked. Jack's visions were meaningless jumbles. The Adrudian left him with nothing but a face that attracted the eyes of curious mill workers and a job that offered him up as dispensable.

The *pull* in Jack's ribs twinged. He'd been able to numb the sensation for a while. He quit Treasurehunting, focused on shoveling ore, dampened the fear that his memory would never return. Still, the itch in his blood remained. Cameron was right; he *was* curious. He suspected the *pull* would stay until he solved the mystery.

Find the House of Matchsticks.

"You want my help," Jack said.

"In a manner of speaking," Cameron replied.

Jack almost laughed, staring at the golden badge, at the

bags beneath Cameron's eyes. The lost expedition haunted Cameron. It was obvious. Cameron hadn't Drunk Adrudian to uncover his memories—yet—but he'd quit Treasurehunting, like Jack. He'd taken the job of Head Inspector, though he clearly didn't want it and had often spoken ill of the Watch. He'd even snubbed his Treasurehunting team.

Cameron met Jack's eyes, lowering his voice to a whisper. "We won't be wrong."

This time, Jack really did laugh. He suppressed the urge to jab a finger into Cameron's chest. "I'm not wrong."

"Even so, Winn's recording is a lead. A better lead than anyone's had since ... well." Cameron paused, and the breeze buffeted his sleeves, wrists appearing and disappearing. "You want to find the House of Matchsticks. So, look for it. Before you poison yourself with Adrudian."

A quiet second passed, then another. Jack couldn't think of anything to say, so he let the silence speak for him. Cameron's mouth spread into a smile.

"Winn's had me speak to the Quandary of Thieves," he said. "They're sending their best to Ar. My friend Neave—you know Neave, from my old Treasurehunting group? She's at Casret Academy bringing back their spy."

Jack forced words out of his mouth. "Sounds like you have a new team. I don't Treasurehunt in teams."

"Jack, all alone." Cameron regarded him closely, brushing the sleeves of his Watchman's coat. "Come with us."

Us, Jack thought.

He took a deep breath, focusing on the cool evening air filling his lungs. His heartbeat slowed. His shoulders unwound.

"If that is a *yes*," Cameron said, grinning, "go east. Tonight. Meet Neave at Casret Academy. She'll tell you everything you need to know."

It was Jack's turn to grimace. He stepped back, widening the space between them. "Why don't *you* go east?"

"I can't leave," Cameron said. "Someone needs to watch the city."

"Someone who better be paying me out of their pretty pockets."

Cameron's lips quirked. He stepped around Jack, strode away, then turned and swept his arms down the sides of his coat. "They *are* pretty, aren't they?"

As Cameron left to catch the ferry to Ar, the last rays of sunshine glimmering off his badge, Jack rolled up his sleeve and raked his fingernails over the back of his burned arm. His insides were humming in the old way, the feeling he used to get before going after something he'd been researching for a long time. The hum of discovery.

If he closed his eyes, he could see Cameron lying unconscious on the ground, blood pooling in the cavity of his chest. He could hear his own voice, barely able to wheeze, memory-blind, screaming for help.

Jack rolled his sleeve down again, pulling it over his raw skin, and returned to the mill. When he slid open the door, a collection of mill workers pushed quickly from the window where they had been watching. He strode past them, glaring into their wide, prying eyes.

"Where's Rhody Charlotte?" Jack said over the mill's thunderous roar. "I'm taking a few days off."

6

BLINKING EYE

ISALINE

It took an hour for Isaline to find and gather firewood, and even longer to collect enough shredded bark and scrubby plants to use as tinder. When she finally made it back to the clearing with an armload of wood and kindling, she was drenched with sweat and covered in dirt. Her stomach grumbled, but she ignored it and hoisted the wood against her chest. She needed a fire before she could think about dinner.

The Thief—Jame—had thankfully kept to his side of the clearing. He was lying in the grass on his back, knitting something that looked like a tea cosy, one foot tapping a silent rhythm in the air. He'd built a fire while she was gone. Pleasant-smelling smoke rose from the flames and unfurled on the breeze. Isaline suppressed a hard scowl as she waddled across the clearing under the weight of her pile of firewood.

Jame's eyes flicked up from his knitting.

"Do you need help?" he asked.

"No." Isaline's firewood went tumbling out of her hands. "I can build a fire, thank you."

Jame sat up and placed his knitting to the side. His hair had absorbed some of the grass, which stuck out all over the back of his head. "I'm going to get some food, then," he announced. He stood and rifled through the pocket of his overcoat, still hanging over the branch of the tree next to him. "I set a few traps this morning."

Isaline massaged her shoulders, not looking at him. "Good for you."

"Lots of rabbits around here." His lips turned up in a good-natured smile. He pulled a folding blade out of his pocket. "Be back in a bit. Make sure the forest doesn't catch fire while I'm gone."

"I don't care," Isaline replied, but he had disappeared into the trees. She shook her head, turning back to her firewood. She didn't need a Quandary Thief to tell her what to do. Building a fire was easy, something she could get done before he returned. When he did, she would go find water.

But the firewood she'd collected was damp and young; it wouldn't light. Isaline hunched over her woodpile, rubbing sticks together until her palms were raw and stinging. No embers. Not even the hope of a spark.

She looked up after what seemed like hours, peering through leaves. The sun had slipped down the sky like a fresh egg yolk. She shivered. Her night was going to be cold without a fire. Worse, she would spend it twenty feet from a perfectly good fire and some kind of survival-master Quandary Thief she had just met.

As if hearing her thoughts, Jame's fire popped, sending a bloom of sparks into the air. Isaline stared at it, an idea forming. Would it be such a bad thing if she lit one of her branches on his fire and brought it back? Her pride would be hurt—but he would never know, and she had to keep an eye on him. Without her in the clearing tonight, he could sneak onto campus. Steal things. A fist wound itself under her ribs.

When I'm a real City Watch, Isaline vowed to herself, *I'll catch* ten *Thieves to make up for this.*

Looking around, Isaline grabbed her driest branch and scuttled to Jame's fire. She held the end of the branch in the flames until it was lit, then hurried back and held the small flame to her ball of tinder. It caught.

Sometime later, Jame came into the clearing with a dead rabbit hanging from his hands. Isaline was sitting cross-legged against a tree, stoking a crackling fire. He laughed, set the rabbit down, and gave her a short applause.

"Glad they're teaching you Watchlings *something* out here," he said.

"Me, too," she muttered in reply.

Jame's fire had solved one of her problems, but still afternoon edged into evening, and Isaline hadn't gone to the stream for a drink.

Her joints had started solidifying into stone, sore and immobile. She stretched her legs and bent her knees, wincing. Jame watched out of the corner of his eye as she got painfully to her feet.

"You look like someone shook you around in a dice box," he said. "Did another Watchling do that to you?"

"Not exactly," Isaline replied. She brushed her hands on the legs of her pants. "I'm going to ..." Her words got stuck, halting halfway out of her mouth. Jame was staring at her now, blinking. She cleared her throat. "Water."

He gave her an angled smile. "Water is good."

Isaline nodded, and continued nodding a few seconds too long. She regretted it instantly. It was charming when Nalissa did it, but it made Isaline look like a bird that had flown into a window.

"You want me to tell you where to go?" Jame asked. He turned back to his knitting, needles *clack-clacking* along the yarn. "The stream's not far, and I found a river the other day."

Isaline made a face and stepped in front of her fire, hiding it from view. "Why are you trying to help me? I don't need your help."

Jame arched an eyebrow at her. "Well, you're just standing there."

"No, I'm not," she replied quickly. To prove it, she

pressed her mouth shut and lurched toward the tree line. "I'm leaving now."

"See you later," he said, chuckling when she pushed a branch so hard it cracked.

Isaline walked north of the clearing, stomping on underbrush. It hadn't taken long for Jame to infuriate her. She'd expected as much from a Quandary Thief. What she hadn't expected were his offers to help. They were insulting, and anyway, a Thief helping a Watchling didn't make any sense.

After a few minutes of searching, the clearing appeared again. Isaline had gone in a circle. Groaning, she cut in a different direction, and got lucky: rounding the side of a tree, she heard the whisper of a little stream. Thin lines of water slipped across the ground, ducking between patches of thorny plants and bright, bobbing flowers. Isaline kneeled and lowered her mouth to the water, taking long, slow drinks. She'd never been sick from drinking stream water on her previous Weeklong Reviews, and hoped she wouldn't be unlucky this time.

When she sat up, her thirst finally quenched, there was something staring at her through the trees.

It was a figure hunched low behind a tree trunk, across the stream and to the left of her. It hadn't been there when Isaline had knelt down. The hair on the back of her neck spiked; whatever it was, it was watching her.

She turned to look at it. "Hello?"

The leaves suddenly shook. The figure slipped out of

sight, disappearing through the trees. Isaline peered at the empty space it left. Water dripped down her chin and she wiped it away. An animal?

She sat still for a moment, waiting, but the figure didn't reappear. Her pendant had slipped out of the front of her top when she'd bent down to drink. Shaking her head, she tucked it back in again.

Stop jumping at shadows, she told herself. *You have enough to worry about.*

She returned to the clearing. Jame had skinned and cleaned the rabbit he had caught, and was sitting next to his fire, roasting the meat. It sizzled and popped, skewered on a long stick extended over the flames. The smoke from the fire mingled with the smell of the cooking rabbit, making Isaline's mouth water.

"That smells ..." she started to say, but then she remembered she wasn't talking to him. Maybe he wasn't talking to her, either, because he didn't look up. Pursing her lips, Isaline marched past him and over to her side of the clearing, where she promptly looked at her pile of firewood and shouted, "*No!*"

Behind her, Jame flipped the cooking rabbit over. A chorus of greasy sizzles and sputters rose.

"Your fire went out," he said matter-of-factly.

Isaline sank to the ground like a deflating balloon.

"Going to get dark soon," he added, as if she didn't know.

Isaline picked through her pile of firewood. It was

charred only in the spot where the flames had caught. The rest was too damp to sustain a fire. Frustrated tears sprang to her eyes, but she didn't have the energy to cry them. She shouldn't have left her fire—it was basic survival, but Jame's appearance had shaken her. Nalissa would have laughed.

Jame sighed. He stood and walked over to her.

"Hey," he said. "At least you still have this."

He patted her stack of extra firewood. Isaline ignored him, staring at her tiny, burned-out fire pit, stomach sinking into the earth. Now there was no way she could start a fire before dark—not if she didn't want to ask Jame to use some of his firewood.

Jame paused, then stuck his hands into his pockets. He returned to his side of the clearing.

"I'll be over here," he said, "if you decide to come visit. Up to you."

ISALINE WASN'T sure how much time passed, but the sun disappeared, and the clearing darkened. Starlings in the oak tree quieted, sidling close to the branches for sleep, and a thick choir of insects took their song's place. Fireflies hovered and weaved among the leaves.

Isaline followed the fireflies with her eyes from her spot at the edge of the clearing. She was slumped against a hard tree root, miserable, with her all-weather jacket draped over her body. A pile of blackberries sat beside her. They were full of seeds, flavorless, and cold.

As evening had come, Isaline had gotten desperate enough to try to make another fire, even with Jame sitting at the other side of the clearing. It hadn't worked, and after a while Isaline was too exhausted and humiliated to continue. She had foraged for some meager berries, then dropped to the ground and resolved to stay still as a rock the entire night.

Across the clearing, the light from Jame's fire made a warm circle, illuminating the grass in shades of yellow and white. He had spent the evening eating his dinner, knitting by the light of the fire, and shooting glances at Isaline. At one point he had called out to her, "Dead yet?" and she had responded with a worn-out shake of her head. At least they had the same inclination for melodrama.

Now, as Isaline snaked her hand outside her jacket to grab a berry, Jame was making little holes in the dirt with his fingers and shaking something from a small paper package into them. He filled the holes with dirt again and sprinkled water from a flask overtop.

Is he planting something? Isaline thought. It seemed cruel. Here she was, dying, and he was doing leisure activities.

She coughed. Jame looked at her sideways.

"You coming to sit by the fire?" he asked.

Isaline said nothing, just stared at him over the top of her jacket.

"It's going to get colder." He turned back to the hole he was refilling with dirt. "I don't know what you're staying over there in the dark for. There's no one from the Academy watching."

His fire crackled and popped, drawing Isaline's eye. It looked warm enough to heat that whole half of the clearing, let alone the spot of bare grass next to it where she could be sitting. The cold rose goosebumps on her arms. If she needed to catch ten Thieves to make up for stealing Jame's fire, how many would she need to catch for sitting with him?

"Besides," Jame continued, pouring some water on the dirt, "I saved some of that rabbit for you."

The memory of how good the rabbit smelled shot into Isaline's brain, lighting it up like a lantern. Her stomach growled. Her resolve broke. She sat up and shook the all-weather jacket from her shoulders. It took only a few seconds to cross the clearing, sit down by the fire, and wrap the jacket around herself again. Heat enveloped her like a hot bath. She sighed, warming her stiff, cold fingers near the flames.

Jame watched her, eyes twinkling in the firelight. "Better? Your hands must have been frozen."

"Much better," Isaline croaked.

He reached around the side of the fire, holding out a stick with a rabbit leg on it. Isaline spared no time biting into the meat. It tasted wonderful, better than anything she'd eaten in years of Weeklong Reviews—including the time she'd cooked her own rabbit, then pulled the flare because she was still hungry.

While she ate, Jame went back to pouring water on the soil and packing it with his hands. His rings sparkled red, blue, and green, like a box of jewels adorning his fingers. Isaline chewed and stared at him across the sputtering fire.

"These will be flowers, if you're wondering," Jame said. He clapped his hands and brushed them on the legs of his pants. "I traded one of my rings for a packet of seeds on my way here. Thought I might as well plant them."

Isaline glanced at his hands. The rings looked expensive. "That doesn't seem like much of a fair trade for you."

Jame shrugged, pocketing the flask of water again. "Probably not." He eyed the stick in her hand. "How was the food?"

The rabbit bone was as clean as Isaline could make it—she had to resist the urge to keep gnawing on the end. "Really good. Thank you." It surprised her how much she meant it. She tossed the stick into the fire, watching as it caught aflame.

Jame sat back and wrapped his arms around his knees. The moss-colored fabric of his coat blended into the trees, making him look like he was melting into the forest. Beneath the fringe of his hair, his eyes were hazel and clever. He seemed honest enough, for a Thief—but she didn't know how she could sit here and talk with him.

"So," Jame said, breaking the silence. He gestured to his face. "How'd you get hurt?"

"I got—" She took a deep breath, five seconds in, five seconds out. Jame waited patiently, resting his bejeweled fingers on his knees. "I got beat up during the Weapons Portion of my exam," she said finally. "The clockwork I sparred with was too strong for me, and I was distracted by ... anyway. I tried to disarm the clockwork, and I failed."

Jame whistled. He picked up a long stick and stoked the fire, pushing coals around in a pile of ashes. "First time failing, then?"

"Yes." Isaline stared at the dirt on her boots. She paused, then added, "Well, the Weapons Portion, anyway."

Jame grinned, passing a hand over his chin. "No need to clarify. I assumed you'd failed this forest part before."

Her face dropped into a frown. "Thanks."

"Really. I've never seen someone struggle so much to find firewood, build a fire, forage for food ..." Jame counted out each on his fingers. "I know the Watch isn't exactly competent, but still. How did you even *get* this far?"

He was smiling, teasing her again, but warmth still bloomed on Isaline's cheeks. "I'm a good fighter," she said, giving him her best impression of a *competent* City Watch. "You don't need to be a good survivalist to work in the city. My Weapons Portion is usually easy."

He raised his eyebrows.

"*Usually*," she said.

Jame laughed and stoked the fire again, sending sparks floating into the air. Isaline examined the shadows on the grass at her feet. It was true—she had failed the easy part of her exam. What would have happened tonight if she hadn't walked into this clearing? Would she have given up and pulled the flare? Shivered in the dark? Jame added another log to the fire, pushing it through the smoke. Quandary Thief or not, he might have saved her future as a City Watch. His requests to help felt like mockery, but here she was, sitting at his fire, and he had saved some of that rabbit for her.

"Why are you helping me, anyway?" Isaline asked him.

He shrugged, the collar of his white shirt bunching. "Better to make friends than enemies, if you're traveling. Never know who you'll meet again."

Isaline didn't know what to say to that. She tugged her pendant out of the front of her top, pressing the pad of her thumb into the keyhole cutout. *Friends.* If she needed to catch fifty Thieves for sitting by Jame's fire, she'd need to take the whole Quandary down to make up for his friendship. Even then, if she passed the Survival Portion, Isaline could never tell Nalissa she had been helped by a Thief.

She cast him a sidelong glance. His features flickered in the firelight, alternating light and shadow. No, Nalissa could never know—even if the Thief in question *was* the type to make her giggle behind her hand.

"Nice pendant," Jame said, pulling her out of her thoughts. He watched her fingers roll it around. "Looks like purpesia."

"Purpesia?" Isaline tucked her chin and looked at it, deep red glinting in the firelight. "Is that some kind of jewel?"

"It's a gemstone. It's only found in the Shute, though. Hard to come by out here." Jame reached into the pocket of his overcoat and rifled around. His pockets must have been leagues deeper than they looked, to hold more than his flask, knitting, and the small knife. "My parents were jewelers. They used to see purpesia in their shop, sometimes, before they died."

"How did they die?" The question came blurting out before Isaline could stop it.

Jame's face went grave, his gaze detaching from her and falling to the grass. "In the takeover. They were killed by clockwork soldiers." He paused, still digging in his pocket. "I hid in the basement."

Isaline bit the inside of her cheek. She'd been ten years old during King Faraday's takeover, still living at the orphanage. Too young to understand that Faraday's clockworks were different from the technology she saw in the shops of Fort Upper, that clockwork soldiers could sense the world around them and be activated by just a voice. She'd been too young to know that clockworks were the perfect soldiers—clean, precise, with no conscience—and that the Justs didn't know how to defeat Faraday's army.

Which meant Jame had been young, too.

He pulled a brass jeweler's loupe from his pocket,

about the length of his thumb. "Your pendant. Can I see it?"

Isaline closed her fingers around the chain. "Can you, a Quandary Thief, see my necklace?"

"Relax, Watchling. I don't want to take it." He smiled at her, the solemn expression washing away. "I might be able to tell you how old it is."

She narrowed her eyes. "I don't think so."

"Suit yourself." He shrugged, unperturbed. "But hey, catch. You can look at it if you want." He tossed the loupe toward her.

Isaline turned the brass loupe over in her hands. There was a notch cut into one side, surrounded by a patch of discoloration from repeated pressing. She pushed her finger into the notch and a round, clear magnifying lens swung out the other side.

"I look through it?" she asked Jame.

"Yeah, you can see the surface of the stone." He added another cut of wood to the fire. "See if it's scratched, or whatever."

"Why would I want to know that?"

"Well ..." He thought about it for a second. "Why wouldn't you?"

Isaline could think of no argument against that, so she brought the loupe to her eye and held out the pendant. She'd had the necklace for as long as she could remember, but had never wondered what the pendant was made of, or what quality it was. Looking close had never crossed her mind, and now it struck her as odd; why hadn't she been more curious about it?

She peered through the loupe. The stone was red—so red it was almost purple—and semi-transparent. Its curvature warped the lines of her palm, glittering. Isaline brought her hand closer. There was something flickering inside the stone, something too faint and slippery to be firelight.

The pendant shimmered. Her lips parted as the stone suddenly shifted from red to black, its color and shine draining away.

Isaline pulled her eyebrows together, confused. She took the loupe from her eye. On her palm, the pendant appeared crimson, like it always had. But when she squinted through the loupe again, it was the color of tar. Something formless was swirling inside it, too, like a school of silver fish wriggling under the surface of a murky sea.

"It's ..." she said, but her sentence died as a round, black spot materialized in the center of the pendant's keyhole cutout.

The spot wasn't part of the stone, but sat in the middle of the keyhole, where Isaline's palm had been showing through only seconds ago. It was glistening, wet, and the size of a button. Surrounding it was a pale, clammy ridge.

Isaline backed her palm away from her face. The spot went with it. Its inky surface had a *depth* to it her mind couldn't understand, as if it weren't a spot at all, but instead a dark window, or lens, or ...

An idea clicked into place. The spot was *looking* at her. An eye.

It blinked.

Isaline's breath caught in her chest. Two maggoty-white eyelids closed and opened around the eye's pupil. A shock went through her, raising the hair on her arms. She was being *seen*, looked at through her own eye, all the way to the back of her skull. She yelped and dropped the jeweler's loupe in her lap.

Jame whirled from where he'd been staring into the forest. "What's wrong?"

Isaline dug at the pendant's chain and pulled it over her head. She threw the whole thing on the grass, scooting backward. "I saw ..." She gulped. Her throat had constricted to the width of a blade of grass. "I thought I saw something looking through the keyhole."

Jame stared at her. "The keyhole ... in the pendant?"

She nodded, but even as she did, she realized how ridiculous it sounded. Another hot flush rose to her cheeks. "I—I'm not sure—" She snatched up the loupe and the pendant again. Bringing the loupe to her eye, she let the pendant dangle in front of the lens.

The stone was red. Red as blood. It circled, slowly, at the end of its chain. The tar-black surface she had seen was gone.

Jame sat watching her, utterly still. Isaline let the loupe fall into her lap again and pressed her palms over her eyes, blocking out the light. The pendant bumped against her forearm.

"It's gone now." She was tired, so tired of this day. "I think I imagined it."

There was a silence, then Jame said, "Hey, it'll be good to get some sleep. You want some water?"

Isaline lowered her hands, bristling against the tone of his voice. She tossed the loupe to him. "No, I don't." She paused, then pulled her knees up to her chest, wrapping her arms around herself. "But ... thanks."

When the moon appeared over the trees, Jame curled up beneath his coat and went to sleep. Isaline stoked the fire, then stretched out and closed her eyes. She didn't know how long it was until she fell asleep, but when she did, she dreamed of rustling branches, a hunched thing looking at them from the dark, and a pitch-black, open eye, staring through the lock of a faraway door.

7

THE HIDDEN BOOK

JACK

Outside the train station, rows of streetlamps lit a long stretch of cobblestones in dim amber light. Jack stepped from the station and into the night air, pulling the ends of his too-big leather jacket close to his body. He shivered. In the packed, dense streets of Fort Upper, it almost never got cool. Still, Jack was used to the sweltering, grease-thick mill, and warming his bones was getting harder to do.

Although it was nearly midnight, Fort Upper's main road was thick with travelers and carriages. Trains left and arrived at Upper Train Station at all hours, a fact for which Jack was grateful. Day trains gave him a headache, and he stood out less on night trains. Tonight, Jack's car had been full of Quandary Thieves, Treasurehunters, and other Adrudian Drinkers. People who didn't look twice at a silent man with blue lines on his face.

Jack jogged down the train station's steps, behind a group of Thieves idly casting around for the eyes of Fort Upper's City Watch. The Thieves were dawdling, so Jack cut to the side and overtook them, glancing at the four of them askance. They were tall, each of them, with overcoats or jackets thrown over their characteristic white collared shirts and close-cut, dark trousers.

Jack straightened the collar of his own shirt, black and flopping above his loosened tie. He hadn't worn this outfit since he'd been on his last successful expedition, the trip before his unlucky attempt to find the House of Matchsticks. Wearing it now felt like a charm, some kind of appeal, but he wasn't sure what he was praying for.

He had changed out of his mill worker's clothes after he'd finished shoveling ore for the day. When he left his room in Lower Village to head for the train, he'd discovered an envelope stuck to his door. Inside was the address of an inn where Cameron had found him a room for the night. The envelope's appearance had rattled Jack, partly because he wasn't expecting to stay in Fort Upper that long, but mostly because it meant Cameron knew where he lived. No one came around to his room, not even the landlord. Not even the men Jack had dated.

The envelope had come with him on the train anyway, tucked inside his jacket, but Jack didn't bother to pull it out. He found the inn not twenty yards from Upper Train Station's steps. Its open door spilled warm light onto the street, slipping over the constant stream of people and carriages funneling toward the station's entrance. Jack slowed his pace and peered through the door at a crowded, jovial-sounding room and a smiling barkeep pouring drinks. The smell of something cooking wafted out and tickled his nose.

Pressing his lips into a line, Jack adjusted his hat and turned away, walking straight past the inn and continuing down the wide street. The first thing he'd done after discovering Cameron's envelope was to write ahead to secure a much cheaper space at the kind of inn that was also a stable. Jack didn't mind sleeping on a hay pile if it meant ignoring Cameron's niceties. The thought gave Jack a particular pleasure.

Fort Upper's main drag carried on past stores, banks, and workshops, all dark and closed for the night. Checking his watch, Jack sidestepped out of the crowd's current and into the mouth of an alleyway. He cast a look at the tall, gray-pillared buildings across the street. He wasn't headed to his room just yet. The night was new, and Fort Upper's library was said to be open late.

Jack peered at the line of buildings across the street, examining one door, then the next. The library should be there, somewhere, but it was hard to discern its entrance from the pillars of the other buildings on either side. The soft Adrudian light absorbed the dust kicked up by the crowd, washing everything in an opaque gray-orange.

As he was about to cross the street, Jack's ears pricked. People and carriages lumbered by with the din of an army, trudging and talking among themselves. But it hadn't been a sound to catch Jack's attention—it had been a feeling. Someone was looking at him.

He searched the mass of people and there she was, a woman with a bright stare fixed on him as she marched by. She held a traveler's trunk in one hand, and had the rumpled appearance of someone who had just disembarked a train. Her clothes were smooth and tailored, her coat done up near her neck, and she was staring openly at Jack with keen eyes.

Just walk by, Jack thought, ignoring the woman and lifting his gaze again to the buildings. He planted his feet, unwilling to enter the road and make it easier for her to intercept him.

But Jack wasn't lucky tonight. The woman eased her way out of the crowd and came toward him.

"I need my future told," was the first thing she said. She was about Jack's height, but seemed to tower over him nonetheless, blocking his view of the other side of the street.

Jack met her stare head-on, then looked away again. Her expression was intent, solid as stone. The other mill workers gave Jack that look, sometimes. It was the look of someone who would rather not be talking to him, but for whatever reason didn't have the choice.

"Well, you can go somewhere else." Jack pulled his back straight, making the joints in his shoulders pop. "I'm not a future-teller."

The woman considered him, then huffed, blowing liquor-scented breath in Jack's face. "Sure, you're not. It's written on your face. I'll give you gold."

Jack's stomach sank. She wasn't going to let him go that easily. He'd had one encounter like this before—someone coming up to him demanding to have their future told. That escape had been narrow, and he wasn't looking for a repeat.

"Your gold does nothing for me," Jack said drily to the woman. "I'm not the Drinker you want." He stepped to the side, trying to duck around the woman's coat and into the crowd, but she extended a long arm, blocking his path.

"Where do you think you're going?" The stony expression on her face had turned down into a snarl. "Tell my future, Blueveins. I know you have the ore."

Jack didn't have any Adrudian, but he figured telling this stranger wouldn't make a difference. The back of his neck tingled, sending a wash down his spine. He didn't want to threaten her.

"There are plenty of Drinkers that will have a vision for you," Jack said. "Just not me." He pressed his hand to his side, a habit more than anything else—he hadn't worn a Treasurehunter's weapons belt in months.

The woman's gaze moved down to his hands, then back up again.

"You're not fooling anyone." She laughed shortly through her nose, sending another waft of breath into Jack's face. "You can't—"

But Jack was already gone, skirting the length of her arm and striding into the crowd. He kept his back and arms rigid, suppressing the urge to glance over his shoulder. She was looking for a fight, and Jack didn't fancy being clobbered by City Watch in a dark alleyway tonight. Especially when there was a library full of books waiting for him across the street.

He waited until he had climbed the steps of the library to look back. As far as Jack could see into the alleyway, it was empty. The woman must have rolled away with the crowd, in search of another Drinker to tell her future. Jack's shoulders relaxed. She wouldn't have to go far—there were Drinkers everywhere, draped in cloaks, pressed into the corners of buildings, blue veins stuck in their cheeks. Jack might share their features, but he didn't belong with them. He wasn't a future-teller, he wasn't a Quandary Thief, and he sure as the stars wasn't a Treasurehunter anymore. He didn't belong anywhere but somewhere in-between.

Exhaling through pursed lips, Jack stepped toward the library.

Fort Upper's library was identical to the other buildings on the street, squashed between thick marble pillars and flanked by an engraved iron door. The door squealed when Jack pulled it open, then swung closed behind him with a rib-rattling *thud*. The sound echoed throughout the vast, empty lobby, drawing the stares of a few sparse patrons. Jack lowered the brim of his hat and slid into the nearest, narrowest aisle of shelves he could find.

Inside the aisles, Adrudian light dripped from ornate, hanging lamps, casting book spines into light and shadow. Jack took a breath in, savoring the smell of parchment, glue, and dust. He'd missed it. Treasurehunters might find fame in the Shute, hunting for artifacts stolen and hidden for generations, but Treasurehunters were *made* in the library, where they researched and drew maps and read histories.

He set off down the aisle, letting his fingertips skim the stiff, fraying spines of the books on either side. Before the House of Matchsticks, Jack had thought of his mind as a kind of library, learning and storing information. He knew better now. Memory kept secrets even Adrudian Milk couldn't unearth. Books held secrets, sure, but only for so long as it took to discover them.

Jack padded down the aisles, purposefully ignoring a section of old newspapers, where a familiar man beamed from the front page on a tall stack. The headline read: *Centuries-Old Ring Found After Shute Expedition by Celebrity Treasurehunter.*

He sighed. Even here, Jack couldn't be rid of Cameron.

Finally, he found the section he was looking for—written histories of the Shute. For Jack, old habits held strong. As a Treasurehunter, he read every book on the Shute in Ar's library archives, as well as in the private library that had belonged to Lillian and Philip Just. Skimming the volumes in front of him, he spied only one unfamiliar title: *Gravel and Lode: Rocks and Gemstones of the Shute.*

He slipped the slim volume from the shelf and stuck it inside his jacket, continuing on.

The library's section on mining was almost non-existent. Instead, Jack followed its sister section on Adrudian around the corner and into an alcove. An old lantern set into the wall splashed the shelves in light. Jack dipped his head, brushing tangles of hair out of his face as he read: *Properties of Adrudian, The Use of Adrudian in Engineering, Adrudian Ore as Light and Energy, Milk of Adrudian and the Human Body.*

His eyes lingered on the last title. Unlike most of his major decisions, Jack's choice to Drink Adrudian had been made without any prior reading. It had been a desperate, night-shrouded impulse that he wished he could forget, if only because it hadn't worked.

Now, hunched over with the spine of this book staring at him, faced with a world of knowledge he hadn't bothered to access, Jack thumbed the book out of the shelf and dropped it into his hand. He let it fall open between his fingers and flipped to a random page in the center.

The visions of the Adrudian Drinker are hard to control, and even harder to predict, Jack read. *Visions can span the future, uncover the past, or prove perfectly meaningless.*

Wrinkling his nose, Jack flipped to another page. *He* could have written that.

Though its visions can be valuable, Milk of Adrudian is toxic to the living body, this page read. *The effect on the host can take years to come to fruition, but Milk will inevitably kill its consumer. In this way, Drinking Adrudian allows the prediction of the future in more ways than one; by consuming Adrudian Milk, the Drinker foretells they will one day die by Adrudian poisoning.*

Jack slapped the book closed. The pages came together with a little puff of dust, making his eyes water. It was nothing he didn't know—and even as he read the words, his mind suppressed them, hiding them away. He didn't need to look at them yet.

As he bent to return the book to its place, a bronze glimmer from within the shelf caught his eye. He paused, then peered into the thin space where the book had been. The light in the alcove was weak, but there it was again: the shine of something metallic at the back of the shelf.

Jack glanced over his shoulder. The aisles were deserted. No one would notice if he did a little digging.

Crouching, he picked books off the shelf three at a time, piling them by his feet. He squinted into the widening shelf space, trying to make out the details of what lay behind. It was long and cylindrical, like a metal bar, but stuck into the back of the shelf so that it sat stiffly at a diagonal.

Jack knew a lever when he saw one. Taking another quick look over his shoulder, he reached into the shelf—it was deep, swallowing his arm up and over his elbow—and pulled the lever down.

Nothing.

He pulled the lever *up*.

Something.

The bar cranked upwards and stayed there. A rumble began, quiet enough to not alert others in the library, but robust enough that Jack could feel it under his feet. He retracted his arm, suddenly afraid the shelf would close in and crush him, some kind of trap.

But it wasn't a trap—it was a door.

Jack stood, taking half a step backward as the rumbling grew, then turned into a swift pattern of *click-click-clicks*. Somewhere, a clockwork mechanism kicked in, pulling the shelves in front of him backward. Jack raised his eyebrows as the shelves retreated a stride's length into the wall, then split in two and slid to the side, like the doors of an elevator, revealing a patch of stale darkness behind.

The clicking of the mechanism stopped, leaving Jack in dusty silence. He gazed into the mouth of the passageway, letting his eyes roam the shadowy space. Empty, maybe. Hidden.

Jack chewed his bottom lip, wrestling with himself. Somewhere outside the library, there was a comfortable hay bed waiting for him, and the promise of a dreamless sleep. He could turn around and find a tavern somewhere. Drink his curiosity away.

But those thoughts were feeble in Jack's mind, hardly loud enough to be heard. His hand brought out his notebook and recorded the location of the door in scratchy print at the top of a blank page. He opened the slats on the lantern set into the wall, reached in, and palmed four tiny rocks of bright Adrudian.

Jack closed his fingers over the Adrudian and held his hand out like a torch. He strode into the darkness.

THE PASSAGEWAY WAS narrow and blank, two rough stone walls stretching straight ahead. Jack's footsteps echoed as he left the library behind, a prickling feeling spreading across his back. A year ago, he wouldn't have hesitated to follow this path. Now, he felt awkward, clumsy, like his limbs were grinding together.

He counted a minute and a half of walking before the corridor ended with a closed door. Jack took off his hat and ran a hand over his scalp. It was cooler than it had been in the library, but he was sweating. The air was dry and smelled like paper mold, as if the passageway led to a much older, abandoned library.

Swallowing, Jack replaced his hat and lifted his palmful of Adrudian up to the door. It had a polished, bronze handle big enough to be pulled with two hands. Beneath the handle, where there should have been a keyhole, there was a round plate of metal, as if someone had replaced the lock with a shiny, flat coin.

The rest of the door contained some sort of clockwork apparatus. A network of interlacing gears spread over the door's face, surrounded by a collection of engraved, golden panels. Jack pushed one of the panels and it shifted, sliding over the face of the door and clicking into place a hand's length to the left. Jack blew out a lungful of breath.

A puzzle door.

Holding the shining Adrudian firmly against his palm, Jack surveyed the door, then began shifting gold panels with both hands, bringing them as close to the gears as he could, until he heard more telltale clicks.

It took him three tries to find the right pattern. When he slid the last panel into place, the gears set into motion, spinning with a smooth, satisfying whir. Jack's heart thrilled despite his unease. Three tries wasn't bad, after a year's worth of nothing.

The gears stopped rotating, and the round metal plate beneath the door's handle slid open to reveal a keyhole. One side of Jack's mouth lifted into a smile. He'd come across more puzzle doors than he could count when he was Treasurehunting—they were a common enough way to hide stolen artifacts—but a puzzle *and* a lock was rare. He'd only come across one other like this: a puzzle deep within the basement of an empty mansion at the topmost point of Ar, years ago.

Jack bent his knees, depositing the glowing Adrudian into a pile by the corner. Pushing his hat back from his forehead, he pulled a long, silvery needle from his pocket.

The memory of the other locked puzzle door was strange to him now, uncertain at the edges but clear as glass in the center. He had used the same lock pick, completed a similar puzzle. It would have been an unremarkable mission if it hadn't been his very first—and if it hadn't been the night he'd met Cameron Agustin.

Both the puzzle and the lock that night had been a struggle. The mansion he'd broken into was said to belong to an esteemed collector, someone who kept everything he ever bought. Even to Jack, a Treasurehunter on his first mission, it was obvious the door led to a vault—a vault he'd hoped would contain just the thing he was looking for.

The vault's puzzle door had been set deep into thick iron and engraved with swirling leaves. Jack had rattled his lock pick so vigorously that when the lock unlatched, it *thunked*, the sound echoing in the vast room behind him.

Jack vividly remembered the sound. His shoulders had come up around his ears. It was late, in one of the wealthiest neighborhoods in Ar. City Watch would be patrolling the street. He'd been lucky not to encounter anyone earlier as he'd lifted himself through a window. He'd held his breath, counting ten seconds, then twenty. Silence. He'd eased the vault door open and slipped through to the other side, leaving the heavy door ajar.

The interior of the vault had been huge, bigger than anything Jack had expected, filled with papers piled up in a state of organized disarray. He could see it in his memory's eye: leaning stacks of folders reaching to the ceiling. Bunches of documents tottering on shelves, lined with dirt and yellowed with age, some of them bound with disintegrating twine. A candle was burning at the other side of the space, throwing long shadows through the forest of shelves and paper. Jack had only a moment to realize there was someone else here before a knife had come up against his throat.

"Watch?" a voice said. Its owner had appeared from the shadows at Jack's side, a tall figure wearing a hooded cloak.

Jack had shaken his head, wincing against the weapon at his neck.

"Good. I don't like Watch," the hooded figure had said. "Thief?"

"No." Jack shrank from the cold sting of the knife. "Treasurehunter."

The figure paused. Their cloak was made of thick, mahogany-colored fabric, gilded at the edges. Expensive. Jack had stared into the shadows under the hood, but couldn't make out any features.

"You're not any Treasurehunter I've seen before," the figure had said. They'd leaned closer, peering at him. Jack had caught a whiff of candle wax—whoever this was, they'd been reading by candlelight long before Jack had arrived. "What's your name?"

"Jack Fael."

"Fye-ell," the figure had repeated. Their voice was a bold tenor. Youthful. Jack would have guessed he and this person were the same age. "What are you looking for, Jack Fael?"

Jack was pressed against a knife—he saw no reason to lie. "A map."

"A map to what?"

"A Golden Chalice." It had been Jack's obsession for weeks. An ancient, forgotten artifact. The figure had tightened their fingers on the knife, waiting for him to continue. "It was stolen by an Ancient Benemournian King," Jack said, clearing his throat. "Is that enough for you? I'm looking for the Chalice. It was stolen and taken into the Shute a thousand years ago."

The figure had paused, then lifted a long hand and threw back their hood, revealing a young man's face. "One thousand and *fifty* years ago, actually." He lowered the knife. "Looks like we're after the same map, Jack Fael."

Jack had stared at him, taking in the pointed nose and the handsome, carved mouth with a wry tilt at its edge. Sharp eyes stared into Jack's—brown, probably, but in the meager light they were two dark pools.

Silence had fallen between them. Jack had no idea what to say; he'd never interacted with another Treasurehunter before, let alone a Treasurehunter looking for the same artifact.

"Did you ... did you find the map?" He'd finally asked, stunned. He stepped away from the door, massaging his neck.

The other Treasurehunter inclined his head and laughed, hair falling over his eyes. He holstered the knife beneath his cloak, revealing a smart black waistcoat and trousers. "Wouldn't you like to know?"

Jack's hands fell to his sides. This man was disarmingly neat-looking. His cloak was fitted as if he'd just walked out of a tailor's, and every hair on his head was perfectly arranged. He was so tidy that a smudge of ink on his index finger glared out of his appearance like a beacon —one tiny flaw. It sent a prickle up Jack's spine. This man had found the map, and had been busy copying it when Jack arrived.

"Who are you, anyway?" Jack had asked, his fingers hovering over his own weapon, holstered beneath the swathes of his moth-eaten cloak. He'd moved his eyes to the far corner of the room, where the lone candle burned on a writing desk spread with documents.

The man passed an ink-smudged hand over his gilded cloak. He leaned against a ceiling-high shelf of folders and crossed his ankles. "I'm a Treasurehunter, like you."

"That's clear enough." Jack took a tiny step to the side. The man was between him and the rest of the vault, but if Jack darted off to the left, he could cut a path through the rows of paper toward the candlelit desk. It would be close, but he might have a chance of getting there first.

"You want to know my name?" the man had asked.

Jack had pulled his eyebrows together. "Do you *want* to tell me your name?"

"Sure." The man had given him a winning smile, as if he'd been waiting for Jack to ask. His white teeth flashed in the dim light. "I'm Cameron Agustin."

Jack's eyes unfocused, the candlelight blurring into a yellow nimbus in the distance. He made a concerted effort to keep his jaw from falling open. Cameron Agustin. Treasurehunting's golden boy. Even Jack, a new Treasurehunter, knew Cameron Agustin's name. The expensive cloak and perfect hair made sense, now; rumor was, Cameron had enough gold to buy a thousand cloaks and haircuts.

He was watching Jack closely, smile wobbling a bit. "You don't seem very impressed."

"Sorry." Jack shrugged, edging a little more to the side. His skin was tingling under Cameron's sharp gaze. "Who's Cameron Agustin?"

Cameron's smile had disappeared. He stood up from the tower of folders, bringing his hand close to his dagger, as if Jack not knowing his name was an attackable offense. "Me," he said. "*I'm* Cameron Agustin. The Treasurehunter. How could ..." He trailed off, spotting the beginnings of Jack's smirk. "You're messing with me."

"Maybe." Jack positioned himself at the opening of a

narrow aisle between stacks of paper and mildewed folders. Cameron had matched his movement, as if they were getting ready to spar. Good. Jack wanted him there, on the other side of a tower of paper. "Where's the map, Cameron?"

"Not here, Jack," Cameron had replied, mimicking Jack's intonation. His wide smile was back. "Gone. I didn't find it."

Jack bent his knees, loosening his calf muscles. "So, you won't mind if I look around."

Cameron tried to keep his expression neutral, but Jack spotted the flick of his eyes in the direction of the candlelit desk. Jack's skin tightened, energy rising in his limbs. The map was here.

"Wait—" Cameron started, but Jack was done talking. He'd leaped forward and pushed the stack of papers between him and Cameron with two open hands. The papers had dropped like a felled tree, one huge mass tipping over onto Cameron, who'd made a grunting sound before disappearing beneath a wave of parchment.

Jack had turned and sprinted down the dusty aisles toward the flickering candle at the far end of the room. He needed to get to the map before Cameron unearthed himself. Cameron might be arrogant, but he wasn't Ar's most revered Treasurehunter for nothing. Jack wasn't sure he could fight him off.

His stomach had flipped when he saw the map on the desk, unrolled with a fresh pot of ink holding down its corner. Jack skidded to a stop, staring at the tangled lines of river and forest painted onto the map with some ancient hand. No wonder Cameron had been here so long. This much detail would take hours to copy.

He'd grabbed the map and rolled it up with shaking hands. Stashing it under his cloak, Jack had retraced his steps, racing down the shadowy aisles and hopping over fallen folders and stacks of parchment. The sounds of shifting paper from near the door made his heart jump against his ribs. He'd prayed Cameron wouldn't be standing in front of the door with his knife drawn.

Panting, he'd emerged at the front of the vault, across from the empty doorway. *Yes.* He'd run for the door, but Cameron's long hand wound itself in the hood of his cloak and pulled. Jack stumbled backward, crying out. He and Cameron had crashed into a shelf, knocking folders to the floor and sending paper and dust flying into the air. Struggling, Jack had managed to wrench himself away. He'd whirled, drawing his knife and pointing it square at Cameron's chest.

Cameron lurched back, palms in the air. "Okay, okay," he'd said. His voice was breathless, husky. Jack had swallowed and renewed his grip on the knife. "So, I found the map."

"So, you did." Jack felt around for the door behind him with one hand. "Did you copy all of it?"

Cameron's eyes had sparkled. He *had* copied all of it.

His teeth shone again in a wide grin. "I guess I'll see you in the Shute, then. At the Chalice."

Jack stood frozen for a moment, then nodded. "I guess you will."

He'd fled through the door and out of the dark mansion.

IN THE LIBRARY, the lock to the secret door clunked and slid open. Jack pocketed the lock pick before gathering his Adrudian, pressing the handle, and slipping inside. As it happened, he and Cameron *had* seen each other in the Shute. Cameron and his team had arrived at the Chalice minutes before Jack, and Cameron had all but stolen the artifact from his hands.

That had been the beginning. The loss of the Golden Chalice had lit a blazing fire inside Jack, a fire that had driven him for years through long nights of reading, perilous expeditions into the Shute, and days searching for treasure after treasure before Cameron got there first.

That is, until the House of Matchsticks. After that expedition, everything had been ruined.

Behind the door, a thin spread of Adrudian light illuminated the corners of a small room. The space was much smaller than Jack had expected, so small he nearly bumped his head on the opposite wall. He took a moment for his eyes to grow accustomed to the dim light, embarrassed despite being alone. He shuddered at what Cameron would say if he knew Jack had picked his way into an empty closet.

The space *was* empty—just four walls and a ceiling with a small Adrudian bulb protruding out of the top. Pocketing his own Adrudian, Jack scanned the walls and felt around with his hands. Nothing. Who would take such pains to hide and lock an empty closet at the back of the library in Fort Upper?

A bead of sweat formed above his right eyebrow, and he brushed it away. For a second there, he had been enjoying himself. Not going through the motions, but really *enjoying* himself. He stood still a moment, letting the feeling drain away, leaving him empty and frowning.

No point in staying if there was nothing to be found. Jack grabbed the door's handle and turned to leave, but stopped when his heel came up against something on the floor. He glanced down at his feet. They were deep in his own shadow from the light above. Bracing himself against the walls on either side, Jack toed around with his boot until he felt the object again, a rectangular, flat thing.

The space was too small for him to bend over, so he crouched and felt around with his hands. His fingertips swept pages and binding. It was a book.

Straightening up, Jack held the book's cover to the tiny light in the ceiling. The title read:

Ancient Benemournian Rituals and Their Uses

His brow furrowed as he peered at the cover. It was

emblazoned with a symbol well-known to Treasurehunters —the symbol of a prosperity ritual. Jack flipped to the table of contents. The chapters didn't *seem* strange or dangerous.

Chapter One: Origins of Ritual-Making

Chapter Two: The Shute as Mystic Site

Chapter Three: Keystones

Chapter Four: Purpesia and Its Properties

Chapter Five: Types of Rituals

Jack scanned the rest of the list, shaking his head. There was nothing here he didn't already know. Ancient Benemournians had conducted rituals in the Shute, pled to the gods for fortune, knowledge, or anything they wanted. Each ritual required an offering, a *keystone*, usually something beautiful or expensive. Something stolen and offered up in exchange for something else.

Rituals were meaningless, in Jack's opinion, and the gods were simple stories. That kind of magic didn't exist, had probably never existed. The keystones, though—they were a Treasurehunter's dream. The Golden Chalice had been a keystone, as were many of the other artifacts Jack had hunted. Keystones were prestige finds, and lucrative, when returned to a paying family that had lost them to a ritual-maker generations ago.

Why would someone hide a single book on Ancient Benemournian rituals behind this locked door? It wasn't even on a shelf.

Jack stood for a moment, flipping through pages, then

came to a decision. He slid the book inside his jacket, tucking it securely where he was sure it wouldn't fall out. It sat next to the book on gemstones, pressed against its slim binding. He pulled his jacket closed and patted the outside, grateful for once to have become a bit bonier since the last time he'd had to steal something.

His cargo secured, Jack left the library, leaving behind the tiny, secret room with its thin Adrudian bulb staring down like an open eye. The book would have to wait. He had a hay bed to find, and a Quandary spy to break out of an academy full of Watch.

8

THE HUNTER

ISALINE

Isaline surfaced from a dream and turned her head toward a chorus of birdsong. Dawn sky peeked through the canopies of trees swaying above her. The starlings fluttered and chattered, shaking their shimmering wings and making the tree branches dance.

Jame sat beneath the oak tree, perched on its bed of roots with his ankles crossed. He was knitting with his pear-colored yarn again, his coat draped over his shoulders like a cloak. He nodded at Isaline as she rolled over and sat up, blinking. The fire had burned all night beside her. To its left was a patch of little green shoots with powder-blue heads pushing up through the ground.

"They're Nightblues, I think," Jame said, walking toward her. He pocketed his knitting, winding his yarn into a ball. "They grow in the dark."

He sprinkled water over top of the shoots with his

flask. Isaline watched his hands as he patted down the dirt, fingers pressing gently around the shoots' small, new leaves. His hair was sticking out at the back of his head, even thicker with grass than it was yesterday.

She cleared her throat. "You didn't know what the seeds were when you bought them?"

"I like surprises." Jame sat down across the fire. The patch of grass where he'd slept was packed down in a rough Jame shape. "Speaking of which ... you look different today."

My face. Isaline touched her cheeks with her fingertips, gingerly patting her skin. Her bruised spots hurt worse than yesterday, but everything felt the right size again.

Jame smiled, brushing dirt from his hands. "Get some river water on there and you'll be good as new. Aside from the bruises." He rocked to his feet, slipping his arms through the sleeves of his overcoat. "Come on, Watchling. Buy you a drink."

They walked to the southeastern part of the forest, Jame taking the lead and Isaline trailing behind, massaging the muscles in her arms. He had been right, the night before: it was better to make friends than to be enemies, at least for now. The thought annoyed her, but if she could tolerate following Jame around for today, she could figure out how to survive for the next five. She needed time to practice being a Country Watch in order to pass her exam.

Jame held a curtain of boughs to the side, clearing a

path for them through two thick trees. "I've been wondering," he said over his shoulder. "If you Watchlings take all your exams in this forest, how do you not know your way around?"

"There's different sections of the forest for students in different years." Isaline pressed her hand on the boughs, hurrying through the trees and letting the branches snap in place behind her. "You might have seen the fences—final year students get most of the training area. They keep the map a secret to make the Survival Portion more difficult."

"Final year students—so, you're graduating." Jame ran a hand over the back of his head, shaking his hair through his fingers. "Where're you going after this?"

Isaline paused, stepping over a rock jutting out of the ground while Jame sidled effortlessly between branches ahead. "I'm going to ... a city somewhere," she said.

Jame turned and gave her a sly grin. "So, you're telling me you're a City Watch?" He chuckled as Isaline's toe came up against a root, sending her stumbling to the side. She waved away the hand he extended to help her. "What city? Ar?"

It wasn't a difficult conclusion to draw. Every City Watchling dreamed of working in Ar, but it took someone really special to be slotted into Ar's Watch forces. Nalissa would have been a shoo-in if she hadn't been drawn to the life of a Country Watch.

Isaline shrugged, hiding a twinge that appeared in her chest. "Ar? Maybe."

Jame clambered up a rocky slant in the forest floor, his pointed boots sending a slide of dirt behind him. "Makes sense," he said. "Lots of Watch in Ar. Not *good* Watch, but ... Watch."

Isaline stopped at the bottom of the slant, one hand raised to brush leaves out of her face. "You've been there before?"

Jame nodded, looking down at her through a snarl of branches. His eyes seemed to twinkle in the midmorning sun, curving into half-moons with his smile. "I grew up there, working at my parents' jewelry shop. I moved south-east when they died a few years ago."

Isaline's heart thumped. She'd never met anyone who had *been* to Ar, let alone someone who grew up there. Distracted, she took the hand he offered, allowing him to help her up the slope. His fingers were soft, the bands of his rings cool on the palm of her hand.

"What's it like?" she asked. The words came tumbling from her mouth of their own accord. "In Ar?"

Jame helped her up until she was standing in front of him. He released her hand. "It's ... high," he said, opening his palms to his sides. His nose was dusted with a blanket of freckles she hadn't noticed before. "Busy. I've smelled better places, too."

The comment brought Isaline up short. She had never stopped to wonder how Ar might smell. She had imagined the mountain, the buildings, the people—but never what the city smelled like. Nalissa had once mentioned that the ocean was supposed to smell of salt. Isaline had unscrewed the lid from a pot of salt in the cafeteria and sniffed inside. It smelled of nothing. She had assumed Ar would smell the same.

Jame's eyes twinkled again, and he strode away through the trees. "Come on. We're almost there."

Ten minutes of walking later, they emerged from the forest onto the shore of a broad, clear river. Smooth rocks dotted the riverbed, bookending weedy green water plants waving and twisting in the deep current. Isaline kneeled beside Jame and they dipped their faces and hair into the sparkling water.

Overhead, a bridge rumbled under the weight of a passing train. Isaline watched the train chug away until it was out of sight, a thousand questions pushing at her chest. She wanted to ask Jame everything. What it had been like growing up in the city. How his parents had come to start a jewelry shop. Why he decided to leave.

But her mouth wouldn't obey her. It had clamped up tighter than a clockwork's fist.

Jame kneeled some ways away, studying a wide strip of mud reaching up from the rushing water. The space between his brows creased, water dripping down the bridge of his nose. He pointed to something on the ground.

"That's a handprint, isn't it?" he said.

Isaline rose and walked beside him. There it was, the print of a hand with its fingers spread out like a spider.

"The fingers are too long," she said, staring at it. The mud was packed in at the base of the print's palm, as if whoever made it had pushed themselves out of the river.

Jame pressed his thumb into the middle of one of the fingers, making a little hole in the mud. "It's fresh, too. Does your school ... keep things in this forest?"

"*Keep* things?" Isaline lifted her head and scanned the riverbank. The ends of her wet hair swept a cold line across her back. "Like what things?"

"Well, *things*. Clockworks. Creatures."

"Aside from squirrels?" She looked back at the print, eyes running over the splay of its fingers. Each one was longer than the length of her whole hand. A creeping feeling skittered across her shoulders. "This isn't the Shute."

"Thankfully." Jame stood, pushing a lock of hair back from his forehead. The water had washed most of the grass from his hair, but there were still a few green blades sticking out the back. Isaline was beginning to think they were there on purpose. "We should keep an eye out."

"Right," she said.

They returned to the clearing. Jame set new traps and prepared food for cooking while Isaline bent over her pile of firewood, trying to build the proper structure for a new fire. She was aware of Jame even more than yesterday, as if he were a streetlamp glaring through a window. His comments about Ar had sent her thoughts spinning. Still, she didn't know what to say, and the longer she stayed silent, the more difficult saying anything became.

Night arrived slowly, the sun tracking its way below the trees in pink and gold. Tonight, Isaline had been able to maintain a small fire and forage for some roots and greens. She sat cross-legged against the trunk of a tree, cracking the end of a large stick into a deadly-looking point, and reciting the City Watch oath in her head. Jame cleared his throat.

"Do you want any of this?" He gestured to the fish he had cooking over the fire.

She did. Its smell was amazing—even better than the rabbit yesterday. But she shook her head and returned to cracking the stick.

"You'll be a passable Country Watch yet." Jame rearranged the fish over the flames. "By the way—I'm leaving tomorrow." He looked up at the darkening sky, as if imagining the train that was going to carry him to the city. "Next time I see you, you'll try to arrest me."

He didn't sound disappointed. It was just the truth. Isaline shifted on the grass, propping one leg beneath her. The flare gun holstered in the loop on her pants had been biting into her thigh.

"We'll see," she said quietly.

"Hm?"

"We'll see."

Jame smiled gently, turning back to his fire. He

propped his ball of yarn close to his knee and started to knit. Next to him, in a patch near his pointed black boots, the Nightblues bobbed their soft, powder-blue heads. Their petals shone in the growing dark.

After falling asleep by her fire, Isaline woke only a few hours into the night. A dream had shaken her—Nalissa, in the shrubs at the base of their dormitory. Hands squeezing her own. Something cold pressed between them. But as she opened her eyes, the dream slipped away, and she turned her head to see that Jame was gone.

She sat up off the ground, dazed, and blinked. The clearing was darker than it had been last night. The moon and stars were blotted out by a mass of black clouds. A cool breeze prickled at her skin and made the grass around her wave. It felt like it might rain, or worse.

Across the clearing, a patch of black shadow sat where Jame's fire should have been. Isaline peered into it. The stalks of the growing Nightblues were visible by the light of her own fire. Next to them was a pile of smoking ashes and firewood that had been burning only hours before. Jame was nowhere to be seen.

Isaline stood up. "Jame?"

There was no response, just the muted humming of insects. She bent down and plucked a branch out of her fire. The end held its flame long enough for her to walk over to Jame's fire pit and see that everything was gone: his overcoat, the small knife he had been using to prepare food, his flask of water for the flowers, and his knitting. The only thing left was an excess ball of pine resin he'd discarded after building his fire.

An uneasy wave washed through her, stiffening the skin at the back of her neck. She stared at his fire pit until the flame on the end of her branch died. Had he left early for the train station? It must have been one o'clock in the morning—far too early to leave for the morning train. But maybe Isaline had slept longer than she thought, and maybe Jame hadn't wanted to say goodbye.

She cast an eye around the clearing. Without Jame's fire, the space felt suddenly huge, a patch of grass the size of a field. Isaline breathed in and out, counting the seconds. Hours ago, the *clack-clack* of his knitting needles had been driving her crazy. This silence was worse. She felt acutely alone.

Shaking her head, Isaline returned to her fire and sat cross-legged in its ring of light. She could have thanked Jame, at least, if he'd woken her up. Thief or not. But maybe it was absurd to want him to have said goodbye—they'd known each other for two days.

She tucked her knees into her chest. Getting back to sleep would be difficult. If she could—

Isaline's thoughts stopped short. She had reached up to tug at the chain of her pendant, but where it should have been, tucked into the collar of her shirt, her fingers found nothing.

Gasping, she felt around her neck and collarbones. Empty. She whirled to look at the spot where she had been sleeping, hoping to see the bronze chain lying there in the dirt. There was nothing. It had disappeared.

No, it had been *stolen.*

Isaline rose, reflexively, like a puppet pulled on a string. Something white-hot and burning rose in her chest, forcing her hands into fists. What had Jame said to her last night?

Next time I see you, you'll try to arrest me.

A thought clicked into place in her mind. He had been planning to take her pendant. Planning since he had first seen it rolling in her fingers the night he had invited her to sit by his fire. The same night she had opened her mouth and told him what had happened at the Academy. Failing her Weapons Portion. She wished she could suck the words back in.

How could she have been so *stupid?*

Adrenaline flooded her veins, jerking her into action. She bent and picked up the branch she had dropped. The ashes of Jame's fire were still smoking. He couldn't have gone far, and they hadn't been back to the river since early afternoon. It was on the way to Fort Upper; he *had* to be stopping for a drink.

With considerable effort, she tore a strip from the inside

of her all-weather jacket and tied it over the end of her branch with shaking hands. Then she rubbed the fabric in the pine resin—good thing Jame had left it behind—and held it into her fire, creating a torch. With her other hand, Isaline grabbed the stick she had broken into a deadly point, just in case.

She set off running into the forest, barreling straight through clusters of thin boughs, cracking them in half and scraping her skin. Even in the suffocating dark, she thought she could find her way.

Nice pendant, Jame had said. *Looks like purpesia.*

Isaline emerged onto the riverbank, panting and branch-scratched, holding the torch aloft. A smatter of rain cooled her forehead, rippling the surface of the rushing water at her feet.

"Jame!" she called out.

No response. The riverbank was empty. The muddy handprint Jame had discovered had dried into a spiderweb of cracks beneath her feet. Overhead, a night train roared past on the bridge, its front-facing Adrudian light cutting through the black sky like a fire-colored shooting star. It bathed the riverbank in a murky orange light. Isaline huffed the smell of Adrudian out of her lungs, hot anger rippling up her back.

"Jame!"

Nothing. Her heart sank. The night was so dark it was leaden. She'd never be able to find him if he was already past the river. The only option would be to cut him off at

Fort Upper—but if she left the training area, she would be disqualified from her Weeklong Review.

Water dripped off her eyelashes. There was nothing she could do; she'd been tricked. Isaline bit her tongue and swallowed a frustrated scream. If she hadn't been so silent —so eager to learn about Ar, but so incapable of talking to him—maybe she would have seen it sooner. Maybe his facade would have cracked, showing what lay underneath.

Her ears pricked. There was something behind her.

She whirled, her torchlight sliding over the glimmer of rolling water. Her pointed stick found nothing in the blackness. Her eyes didn't, either—only the dark figures of trees looming like sentinels, and the tenebrous forms of rocks and shrubs.

"Jame?" she said. Her voice came out a weak impression of her earlier call. "Jame, is that—"

A hand clamped over her mouth from behind. Isaline cried out, her arms going rigid. Her torch fell from her fingers into the river, winking out into darkness.

"*Watchling*," Jame's voice whispered in her ear. "You have to get off the riverbank, come on."

The hand over her mouth was soft, the metallic bands of rings pushing gently into her cheek. A shock ran up the back of Isaline's arms; it *was* Jame. She thrust her elbow backward, hitting him hard in the stomach. He made an abrupt sound of surprise, breath whooshing over her shoulder, and his hold loosened.

"Get—*off*—me." Isaline wrenched out of his grip. He

stumbled, barely visible in the dim light, holding one hand over his stomach. She renewed her hold on the pointed stick. "I thought I'd find you here."

Jame bent at the middle, groaning. "Your elbow's so *sharp*," he wheezed.

Isaline planted her hand squarely in the middle of his chest and shoved him, backing him up against a tree some ways from the river. He didn't resist, just fanned his arms out to the side. "You took it, didn't you?" She raised her stick, letting its point press into his throat. Her voice lowered. "Give it back."

Jame stared at her, his eyes so wide she could see the whites all around his irises. "Give what back? We shouldn't stay here—"

"My pendant," she said. Her voice faltered. She hadn't thought about what she was going to say to him. "You've been—you've been planning—"

"Planning? To do what? Planning to keep us from getting killed while we sleep?"

Isaline squinted at him, trying to see his face in the dim light. His lips were parted in a silent gasp, his hair sticking up on one side. He looked as flabbergasted as if she'd spontaneously grown a third arm. A niggle of uncertainty rose in her stomach. "Planning ... to steal from me." She blinked. "Wait, what are you talking about?"

His expression dropped into something inscrutable. She felt his chest tense under her hand. "You think I took something of yours." It was a statement, not a question. "That keyhole necklace."

Isaline bunched the collar of his white shirt in her fingers. She was grateful for the darkness growing in the wake of the train's light; they were close enough for their breaths to collide. "It's my fault, really," she said. "You *seem* nice, but ... you can't help what you've been trained to do."

Jame let out a hard, humorless laugh. "Neither can you, apparently."

"What's that supposed to mean?"

He lifted his arms, palms up and gesturing at the forest around them. "I never asked to meet you, Watchling. You just wandered into my clearing and never left."

"You wandered into my *Academy* and never left," she replied. "Why are you—" He edged away from the tree, trying to slip out of her grasp. She shoved him again, hard, and he flattened his back against the trunk. "Why are you here, really? Don't tell me you're just passing through. I don't believe you."

Jame pursed his lips. "I'm not here to steal your things, if that's what you're implying."

She didn't respond, just pushed the stick a little harder against him. His shoulders stiffened, then slumped back against the tree. "Fine. Not that it concerns you, but I've been writing to someone at the Academy. A student. I heard maybe she'd be out here on her exam while I was passing through."

It was Isaline's turn to laugh. "I don't know a single Watchling that would write to someone like you."

"That's right," Jame said. "You don't."

Isaline had no idea how to respond to that. Above them, the train's lamp had shrunk to a bright pinhead in the distance, leaving them in darkness. She paused, grinding her teeth together. Jame shifted under her grip.

"You're shaking," he observed.

She was. Her arms had gone soft, jelly-like. This wasn't going the way she'd envisioned. Her City Watch training had taught her to detain lawbreakers, not negotiate. She didn't know what to say to make him give up the necklace. She could check his pockets herself, but *that* thought was almost more overwhelming than losing the pendant. When she clutched his collar, the back of her hand tingled where it met the warmth of his chest.

"If we're going to keep doing this, can we at least go back into the forest?" Jame whispered. He peered over the top of her head toward the river. "We're not safe here."

Isaline's eyebrows pulled together, her grip on the pointed stick wobbling. "What do you mean?"

"You haven't asked me why I'm at the river yet—why I grabbed you." He gave her a level look. "Sorry about that. But I guess we're even now." His eyes lifted over her head again, scanning the riverbank. "Something came into our clearing tonight. It woke me up; I didn't get a good look at it, but I heard it. I followed it here."

"An animal?"

Jame shook his head. "Not even close. It made that handprint, I'm sure of it." They both glanced toward the riverbank, where the dried print was moistening in the sprinkling rain. "It ... slid into the river. A few minutes before you got here."

The sudden blare of a train whistle cut through the silence, making both of them jump. A new point of orange light appeared in the sky—another train chugging toward them across the bridge overhead. She twisted her fingers deeper in the collar of Jame's shirt.

"Stop lying," she said.

As the light grew, Jame's face came into better focus. His eyes were serious, the space between his brows pinched. Much like when they had first met, something in his expression told her he was telling the truth. Her grip on his shirt loosened as he met her gaze with an earnest look.

"I'm not lying." His fingertips whispered at her elbow, drawing her arm away from his chest. She released his collar, easing the knot under her shoulder blade. "I wouldn't take your pendant. We're ... friends."

"Friends," Isaline repeated. Even in the faint light, she could tell they were standing too close. She shuffled backward, keeping the pointed stick against the hollow of his throat. "But if you didn't take my pendant, where is it?"

"*Going back where it belongs*," someone said.

A cold chill pierced Isaline's spine. That hadn't been Jame's voice. She yelped and spun around, accidentally scraping the point of her stick across Jame's collarbone, stinging his skin. He gasped and flung himself back against the tree, eyes darting everywhere in the dim light.

"I tire of waiting for you to wake."

The voice was low, whispering, but loud enough to drill into Isaline's ears. She swung the pointed stick around in front of her, but there was nothing to hit. The riverbank was vacant: nothing but rushing water, columns of pine trees reaching like giants, and another train, approaching on the bridge and casting everything in its Adrudian glow.

"Show yourself," Isaline said. A fresh wave of adrenaline surged through her, sharpening her eyesight. She peered into the trees at the river's edge, gaze running over every trunk and stone.

Jame drew close beside her, pressing the palm of his hand over the scrape on his collarbone. His chest rose and fell at a gallop. "The river," he said, raising his voice over the thundering train advancing above them. "It's in the river, remember?"

As if in answer, the water bubbled suddenly, in a patch straight ahead of where they stood. Both Isaline and Jame tensed, staring open-mouthed as two hands with salt-white fingers emerged, squelching up onto the bank like thick, wet snakes. Each finger was too long and multi-knuckled, bending and contracting in the mud. The hands were followed by wrists, then bony arms with pale skin stretched over slug-like, quivering biceps.

"That's it," Jame said under his breath. The ground had started to rumble, dust raining from the shuddering bridge overhead. He grazed his fingertips over Isaline's shoulder. "The thing that was in our clearing. What ... is it?"

Isaline didn't know, but even if she did, her voice had shrunk and buried itself deep in her throat. She blinked, and blinked again, her mind trying and failing to understand the sight of the head appearing out of the water. It was mostly bald, humanoid, with fishy skin and patches of colorless hair. The creature slithered onto the riverbank face-down, so she couldn't see its facial features—a fact for which she was absurdly grateful.

"*I have been waiting*," it said. Its voice was dry, inhuman, like the scratch of dead leaves. The sound didn't seem to come from its body, but appeared inside her head, as if it were curled within her ear canal.

Isaline's tongue glued to the top of her mouth. She swallowed and somehow found her voice. "Who are you?"

"*A hunter.*" It coiled up on the bank, its torso heaving slowly out of the river. Isaline's thoughts plummeted in a free fall. The slimy, porcelain torso had no end; it kept coming, writhing out of the water, long and dripping like the body of a man-sized worm. With a sound like a heavy sack being dragged through mud, it coiled and coiled until it had fully emerged, its body tapering, legless.

Isaline bit down a scream. Her own voice echoed in her mind: *This isn't the Shute.* She'd said as much to Jame this morning, hadn't she? Why had this creature come here, out of the ancient forest, the only place in Benemourne where monsters were said to exist?

Jame had been thinking the same thing. He stepped forward—only half a foot's length, but Isaline had to suppress the urge to pull him back. "A hunter," he said. "Trading one forest for another, are we?"

The creature's head lolled limp on its shoulders, its face hidden by the winding of its body. "*I do not come from that place.*" Its pale skin glistened orange in the growing light—the approaching train would be passing overhead any minute. "*I was sent from Ar. Sent to retrieve the lock that was taken. I will kill the one who kept it.*"

Isaline's hand shot up to her collar. The pendant was gone, and this creature had said *kill.* Why hadn't it killed them while they were sleeping? Was it lying to them?

The creature rocked its face back and forth on its body, offering no explanation. She still couldn't see its features, but the shadow of something caught her eye: a dark knot of fabric sitting at the crown of its head. Isaline stared at it, unable to identify what it was, but then it came to her.

The thing was wearing a blindfold.

There was something wrong with the eyes.

"*Enough talk, now,*" the creature breathed. Its body undulated, muscles rippling beneath slimy skin. "*You will die tonight.*"

The train had finally reached them, its roaring iron

cars making the bridge tremble and shake. The river glittered in the light from the train's coppery headlamp. Glancing up, Isaline sucked Adrudian-thick air through her teeth. It was light now, but as soon as the train chugged into the distance, they would be in the dark again. In the dark with this *thing*, and the light was already waning.

"Jame," she said, "get behind me."

He turned to her, his eyes as wide as medallions. "You're going to fight it?"

"Do you see a better option?"

"Running—we should run. Thieves don't exactly get combat training, you know."

Isaline shook her head. "But we don't have a torch. It'll catch us in the dark. Just ... let me handle it."

The creature uncoiled, tensing and pulling, ready to strike. Goosebumps blanketed Isaline's arms. Even with its face in the mud, she could feel it looking at her, watching her every move. She bent her knees and raised the stick, her heart hammering. Its skin looked slimy, supple, but Isaline guessed it would be thick and difficult to pierce. She would have to aim for its head, neck, or between its shoulders: the part of its body that looked like a human before morphing into a snake. When it stood up, it would probably be the height of a tall man. If it *could* stand up.

Jame remained rooted to the spot, staring slack-jawed as the creature scrunched its lower half, preparing to attack. Isaline brushed at him with the back of her arm, drawing him behind her.

Wait, she told herself.

Wait.

Wait.

Now.

The creature lunged, its snake-like body pushing its human torso face-down across the ground. Isaline jabbed down with the stick, narrowly missing the wrist of one spidery hand. It pulled back and rushed her again, this time dodging the point of her weapon and wriggling up to her legs. Surprised, she lurched backward, crashing into Jame, but there was no time to thrust her weapon down in defense. The creature wrapped its long fingers around her ankles and yanked.

Isaline's feet slipped out from under her, and the ground fell away. She would have dropped hard and smacked her head if it hadn't been for Jame grabbing her under the arms and heaving her up. The creature kept hold of her ankles and wrenched itself backward, its drooping head swaying on its shoulders.

The world tilted. She was looking straight up at the coal-black sky; she had been stretched horizontal, suspended between the creature and Jame, like a rope being pulled taut. Her lungs flattened, throat on fire as she flailed, pointed stick tipping from her hand. Wheezing half-screams escaped her mouth.

It's got me, her mind shrieked. *Oh no, oh no, it's going to pull me, it's going to take me into the river ...*

Panicking, Isaline bent her knee and kicked out with

her right foot. Her ankle slipped from the creature's hold. She kicked again, aiming for its slumping head. Her heel connected with its scalp, and it made a sound like a hissing reptile. The long fingers released their grip on her other ankle. Her legs fell to the ground.

Jame heaved her against him, pressing the nape of her neck against his stomach. The monster slithered close—she tried to kick it, but it was too fast. It put its hands on the ground on either side of her scrambling feet and pushed itself up on its arms, raising the saggy torso of its body over her own. Isaline saw the muscles of its neck squeeze, engaging as it lifted its hanging head, and now she truly screamed, for its face was not a man's face at all.

The creature brought its face—or what passed for its face—so close she could smell its sour breath, issuing out of a once-human nose long rotted away. Its smile was lipless, black like rot, far too wide, far too toothy.

"*You …*" it said. "*You … you … you …*"

Something was moving under the front of its blindfold. Two lumps skittering side to side like a pair of cockroaches crawling beneath thin fabric.

It's going to take off the blindfold and look at me. Isaline screamed again, trying and failing to get her footing. *It's going to look at me and I'll never forget what I see, I'll die if I see its eyes, no no no.*

"Jame!" she shrieked.

Her voice seemed to break him out of a daze. Grunting, he heaved his elbows under her arms and dragged her backward, skirting the tree they had been pressed against. The monster tried to snatch her ankle again but missed, its worming fingers grasping at air.

"You will not escape me, Watchling."

The grass at the edge of the forest had better purchase for Isaline's boots. Jame released her arms, stepping to the side as she stood up on trembling legs. Rain speckled her forehead. She glanced upward. The train had passed and was shrinking into the distance—they had only a minute of light left, or less. The river's edge was swathed in shadows, the tips of the trees invisible against the black sky.

"Here we go," she murmured, and sprinted toward the creature, scooping the pointed stick from the ground.

She leaped and jabbed at the space between the creature's shoulders, but it slid to the side and dodged out of her path. Pivoting, Isaline struck downward. The point of the stick raked through its glistening back, splitting the skin. Orange slime burst out and sprayed her legs, coating the tops of her boots. The creature screeched, enraged, and reached for her hand. Its fingers caught the stick and tossed it away.

Time seemed to slow as the stick flew through the air. It soared across the mud and plopped into the river, lost amid the black water. Isaline's knees nearly buckled. She couldn't fight this thing with her hands.

The creature reached for her. She stumbled backward, coming up against a tree. The train's light dimmed further.

Isaline's vision grayed as the creature slid forward, hands speeding over the ground, aiming for her legs.

A shadow darted in front of her—Jame, brandishing his cooking knife. He stabbed downwards once, twice, three times, but the creature knocked the blade away with its bony arms. It slithered toward Jame, away from Isaline, and wrapped its fingers around his legs, pulling him off his feet. Mud sprayed in Isaline's face, followed by the sound of Jame being dragged across the ground. Isaline's breath trapped itself in her throat. It was almost too dark to see, and the creature was pulling Jame into the river.

"No!" Isaline staggered in the dark, splashing into the water, bending and feeling around with her hands. The river was ice cold, chilling her down to her bones and setting her teeth on edge. She waded blindly until Jame's muffled cries and a thunderous splash sent her barreling to the right, water soaking under her all-weather jacket and turning her top into a wet rag.

She followed Jame's voice until her fingers swept the fabric of his overcoat at the edge of the river. He was splashing frantically, trying to pull himself back up onto the riverbank. Isaline grabbed his hands and heaved, pulling him above water, but the creature tugged him down again. A dry, grating laugh resounded in her head.

"Don't move, girl. He will be dead before you can save him," the creature said. Isaline froze, her joints locking at the sound of its voice. She could just make out its head

splitting the rushing water at Jame's feet, an arm's length away. "*He will be dead before you try.*"

The train's light winked out. Isaline closed her eyes and opened them again. Something shiny had caught her attention a split-second before the light vanished.

"*Let him die. Let him ... let him ...*"

The keyhole pendant. It winked at the hollow of the creature's throat, tucked between two flaps of slimy white skin. An image broke into Isaline's mind: this creature slithering into the darkened clearing, stretching out its long fingers, lifting the necklace over her head as she slept next to the fire.

As Jame slept next to the fire.

Something inside Isaline twisted. Her training, already slipping, dropped away completely. Suddenly, she didn't care about the Weeklong Review. She didn't care about Casret Academy. She didn't care about the City Watch.

All she thought to do was save him.

She reached down, reached back up again, and pulled the trigger on the flare.

9

MURMURATION
THE COLLECTOR

The flare popped into the night sky above the Collector and Caladrius. Lavender, sparkling like a firework, it unfurled wide in the air. A few moments later, a sharp *crack* sounded out.

The Collector pushed his hat snug onto his head and peered at the light spreading out over the dark, gathering clouds. Caladrius tittered, shifting from one foot to the other. They had stopped on a small outcropping of rock overlooking a valley, where the land dipped into a slight bowl. The canopies of trees washed and waved in the darkness. Behind them, through the forest, the tall stone buildings of Casret Watch Academy shone.

Squinting, the Collector examined the sparkling purple light until it winked out, leaving a smoke print in its wake. Caladrius chirped and fluttered off his shoulder, lifting through the air and settling onto a high branch.

From her perch, she stared in the flare's direction, her head tipping back and forth.

"What do you see?" A crease gathered the corners of the Collector's mouth. Since they had traveled from Ar, Caladrius had been unusually spirited: tweeting, chirping, and flitting all around, acting more like a hummingbird than a starling. It was the Justs who had given her such energy—he knew it. He glanced at them, their slow swirl in the Jar of Lights pressing an uneasy weight to his chest.

Caladrius whistled. She flew back to his shoulder and tugged at the fabric of his coat with her talons, urging him through the trees toward the flare. The Collector hesitated. Before the flare had erupted in the night sky, she had been leading him the opposite way, toward Casret Academy.

"Are you sure?" The Collector tucked his chin to look at her. "I thought that we—"

She chattered and nipped him on the ear. Not hard enough to hurt, but enough to give him the impression of hurting. He smiled despite the tangle of nerves in his stomach.

"Fine. If you say so."

She leaped off his shoulder and flew through the trees, a ball of darkness cut with the points of stars. The Collector picked up the Jar of Lights and followed, gliding along the high breeze, passing through tree trunks, berry bushes, and underbrush. The air was thick with an impending rainstorm.

A smattering of rain was falling when he reached the bank of a broad river stretching beneath one of Fort Upper's soaring train bridges. He stepped between the trunks of two swaying, creaking trees behind Caladrius. Ahead of them, water rushed in a wide, dim ribbon, severed at its edge by three figures struggling and splashing near the riverbank.

"What happened here?" he said aloud, though no one but Caladrius could hear him.

A boy, wearing a green overcoat blackened with water, dragged himself from the river and slumped on his hands and knees, retching. Not far from him, a girl about the same age stood knee-deep in the river, pointing a small, engraved flare gun in the air with her right hand. Her left hand was clenched into a fist at her side.

In the stretch of water between them, the Collector saw something his mind consolidated into a large fish lifting its head out of the river. It bobbed, not really fish-like at all, slipping downriver with the current.

"*I will hunt you,*" it said. The Collector shuddered as its voice rattled inside his head like an echo trapped in a canyon. He'd heard it before—it was the second voice on Winn Just's recording. The voice speaking to the King. "*Wherever you go, I will follow you.*"

The girl said nothing. She stood, bracing herself against the surging water, and waited while the creature slipped away. In a few moments, its head had submerged and was gone.

Caladrius whistled. She hopped onto the Collector's shoulder and clamped his coat with her talons, staring transfixed at the girl with the flare gun in her hand. To the Collector's eye, the girl looked unassuming: beige skin purpling with bruises; a defined cupid's bow stretched in a frown; hair in a tangled mess of curls; wide, dark eyes.

Then she loosened her left fist. Strings of slime stretched between her fingers, as if she'd stuck her hand into a pot of glue. Something shiny fell through: a long, bronze chain with a red pendant at the end. The lock swung back and forth, skimming the surface of the water flowing around her legs. She bent and washed her hand in the water, rubbing the pendant between her thumb and forefinger.

The Collector's body numbed. He looked at the girl's face, studied it, and in an instant, he was transported back sixteen years. Smoke blanketed the night sky. The hot tang of melting metal and death spread out like a poison. Here the child was, grown out of the bundle her mother had tucked against her chest. She looked utterly different from when the Collector had seen that small hand, clutching at the air, disappearing into the distance—disappearing thanks to his pushing the edge of her rocking rowboat.

This girl is alive because of me.

The Collector had the troubling urge to take a deep breath. Breathing was unnecessary for him, far too human a gesture. He forced the urge down.

Wiping the pendant on the front of her pants, the girl

waded from the river. She kneeled beside the boy with the green coat, feeling out with her hands until she touched the soles of his boots. The Collector drifted closer, straining to hear above the roaring water.

"Jame," the girl said in a low voice. "Are you okay? You have to go."

The boy coughed, spitting water onto the mud. The hand clutching his throat was bejeweled with precious stones, vibrant against his skin, which was pale enough to gleam wet in the darkness. He sat up on his knees and took big gasps of air. When he tried to say something, his voice came out a rasp.

"The examiners will be coming." The girl looked around in the darkness. "You have to go, or you'll get caught. Come on."

She stood, pressing her fingers to the inside of his wrist. The boy called Jame took her hand and pushed himself off the ground, his legs wobbly. The girl helped him walk to the forest, one hand extended to keep them from bumping into trees. At the tree line, near the space between two trunks, she released his hand.

"I—" The girl rubbed her palm on the soaked forearm of her jacket. "I feel bad about—"

Jame stopped her short, turning suddenly to pull her into a hug. They stood there for a moment, one of his hands resting at the nape of her neck. Then he slipped between the trees and was gone.

The girl from the boat stood rooted in place. Her arms

were straight as boards at her sides, down to her fingers, which were spread out as if she'd been frozen. The red pendant turned circles in the air below where its chain was wrapped around her wrist.

"Caladrius," the Collector said. He brushed his fingertips over the brim of his hat. "She kept it, all these years."

The bird chirped, as if to say, *Of course she did.*

At the edge of the forest, the girl sat in the mud, her body shaking from being soaked in the frigid river. Silently, the Collector shuffled to the side and waited, skimming the water with the bottoms of his feet.

After a breadth of quiet minutes, footsteps and the sound of breaking branches emerged from within the forest. The girl tossed the bronze chain around her neck and tucked the pendant into the front of her shirt. Standing, she squared her shoulders and turned to face the oncoming noises.

Five people emerged from the tree line. The first was a man with spectacles and a clipboard, the Headmaster of Casret Academy. He was wearing his dressing gown and a sour expression, obviously unhappy about being roused in the middle of the night. Next to him was a tall woman wearing all black. An orange pin glittered at her lapel. A Shute Treasurehunter.

The three others were professors wearing overcoats over their nightclothes. Rain speckled dark spots on the fabric of their coats and bright spots in their hair. Each of them held an Adrudian flashlight, orange beams cutting through the night. They trained them directly on the girl from the boat, making her gasp and shade her eyes.

The Headmaster glanced at his clipboard, then pressed it to his chest to shield it from the rain. "Your Survival Portion has now ended," he said. "Couldn't wait until morning, I suppose?"

"N-no," the girl said through chattering teeth.

The Headmaster glanced at the clipboard again, pushing his glasses to the tip of his nose. "You have failed your Weeklong Review."

She nodded, trembling. "I know."

"For stars' sake, stop pointing those at her," the Shute Treasurehunter said. She smacked the nearest flashlight away. "Can't you see she's in shock?" The professors glowered, but shifted their flashlights to the side. The girl from the boat lowered her hand, wincing under the intent stare of the Treasurehunter. "What made you pull the flare?"

The girl hesitated, then seemed to come to a decision. "There's a monster in the training area," she said. She found the courage to look the Treasurehunter square in the eye. "It attacked me. I would have died if I hadn't pulled it."

Something flickered across the Treasurehunter's face. She straightened up.

"Preposterous." The Headmaster clicked his tongue. "We will discuss it at the Academy, though I can assure you this will not be sufficient to pass your exam." He removed his spectacles and wiped them on the front of his dressing gown. "You will be required to leave school premises first thing tomorrow."

Thunder clapped. The rain was coming down in earnest now, big wet drops running down the bark of trees and turning the riverbank into a muddy soup. The Headmaster pressed his clipboard more firmly against his body.

"Now, let's get out of this infernal weather," he said, taking the lead into the forest, "before we all catch our deaths."

The professors waited for him to pass, then pulled their overcoats around themselves and followed, their lights shrinking behind the trees.

The girl from the boat glanced one last time at the place where Jame had left the clearing. She trudged toward the tree line, shoulders quaking. The Shute Treasurehunter paused, one hand holding a tree branch to the side. She looked at the girl over her shoulder.

"Took you long enough." The Treasurehunter smiled, lined lips parting conspiratorially. "We've been waiting."

The girl stared at her. "What?"

But the Treasurehunter was already gone, branches swept to the side and enveloped by darkness.

The thickening rain fell through the Collector's body and joined the river water below his feet.

"She's alive," he said to Caladrius. It was a useless statement, but he couldn't think of anything else to say.

Caladrius sang and clawed the fabric of his coat in a bunch. She nuzzled his jaw with the top of her head, a warm spot below his earlobe.

"Aren't you worried?" The Collector dropped the Jar of Lights on the river's surface and wrung his hands together. "We—I made a *choice*, Cal. With a consequence. We don't make choices ... humans do."

She whistled, hopped off his shoulder, and flew in circles around his head. He looked up at her. The one-way barrier to their communication had never seemed so solid. Caladrius had always understood his language, but the Collector had never been fully able to decipher her bird noises. He had often wished to speak with her plainly, if only to learn her thoughts about trivial matters. This was different. He couldn't help but feel she knew something he didn't—something given to her by Lillian and Philip Just. The thought turned his middle into a churning, uncomfortable mass.

"I don't understand," was all he could say. He picked up the Jar of Lights so the space around Caladrius was bathed in bright, sky-blue light. "It's not right. I should have—I should have just let the boat stay. I should have let her die."

Caladrius chirped sharply, turning in the air and looking at him with reproach.

"Well, what would you have me do?" he asked.

She flapped her wings, a sure encouragement to follow her. This time, the Collector didn't hesitate. He walked off the river and through the dark trees, his heartbeat pulsing beneath his skin.

Caladrius led him to a round, grassy clearing within the forest. Two fire pits had been assembled five or six steps apart, ashen and dark in the smothering rain. The Collector peered beside the closest pit, examining a patch of blue flowers drinking the dark. One of them had been planting Nightblues. He wondered if it had been the boy in the green coat, Jame, or the girl from the rowboat.

At the edge of the clearing was a towering oak tree spread with a gnarled blanket of roots. Caladrius flitted up its large, twisting branches, her starry silhouette disappearing into a cluster of shadowy leaves. The Collector followed, as he always did, picking his way over the bed of roots. She tittered at him from above.

"I'm coming, I'm coming." The Collector craned upwards. The tree loomed over him, the inside of its dome a dark abyss. Caladrius chirped from within it, so the Collector hooked the Jar of Lights over his elbow and climbed, hand over hand and foot over foot, all the way to the canopy.

The oak tree was the tallest he'd seen in the Academy's training area. As the Collector climbed, he was surprised to find bunches of black feathers roosting—starlings asleep in the dark. Hundreds of them. The blue glow from the Jar of Lights slid over their sleeping forms, orange beaks tucked, shiny, black feathers ruffled. When he reached the top, he sat on a branch next to Caladrius, who was perched in between leaves.

The training area stretched out all around them, a vast plain of rustling green beneath a stormy sky. Rain fell in sheets, striking the mounds of the trees and making them ripple like the surface of the ocean. Caladrius whistled.

"So?" The Collector stared at her, a spot of stars soaking in the darkness. She looked tiny within the vast landscape of the world. "What are you showing me?"

She sang again, louder this time, and the tree suddenly came to life. The Collector turned to stone as the sleeping starlings below stirred all at once, shaking their bodies, making the branches of the tree vibrate. A rush of trills sounded out—they were speaking to each other. He looked down through the leaves and saw a mass of dark feathers and bright beaks undulating.

"Caladrius ..." he started, but his words were lost as the starlings took flight, all together, rising as if pulled on strings from their branches and into the sky. Several of them passed straight through the Collector, whooshing through his body like arrows shot from a bow. He pulled the Jar of Lights close to him, afraid to drop it in the tumult.

The birds collected above the tree in a rippling cloud. The Collector looked down to Caladrius, mouth open, but her branch was empty. She had flown up there, too, with the rest of them, a spot of pinpricked stars in the multitude. His heart stuttered. There were so many of them—what if Caladrius was lost among the crowd? What if she lost sight of the ground?

The Collector could do nothing but watch as the birds began to fly back and forth in a wave, gathering and spreading in the air, a living mirror of the storm clouds above them. They swirled, dove, sank, and rose, Caladrius among them, like a small galaxy soaring. Each bird flew as if tethered to the next; if one changed direction, so did its neighbors and their neighbors, creating a ripple that spread and changed like an echo. The Collector had the abrupt impression of a wavelet from a tiny rowboat gliding into the distance. It was a great chain of cause and effect that linked the starlings together.

The birds made no sound save for the constant, immense susurration of their wings. They dipped, soared, and were utterly silent, letting the murmuration's rhythm take over and guide their flight. Caladrius, however, was singing as she flew among them, a song so bright and playful the Collector's concern for her washed away. He found himself laughing, holding the Jar of Lights to his chest, face turned open to the rain.

Finally, the murmuration waned. Birds dropped in tandem to the tree, settling like a blanket over its branches. The Collector held out his hand, the laughter of a moment ago ebbing with the murmuration's rhythm. Caladrius floated down in a spiral. The last of her song quieted. She perched on the palm of his hand.

"Quite a show," he said to her.

She whistled softly, ruffling her feathers. Her body pulsed in and out—breathing. Something she had never done before. Ice crept along the Collector's spine, but he forced his mouth into a smile and brought Caladrius close to his face. She pressed the top of her head against his forehead.

"They may live like that," he said, making his voice serious. "Together in a cloud. Converging." He brought his hand out to her, running his fingertip gently over her feathers. "But I'm not a bird, Caladrius, and neither are you. We don't belong in a world of choices and consequences. We are apart. We are down here, while they are ..." The Collector paused, searching the roiling, wet sky. "They are somewhere we can't go."

Caladrius made no sound. She stared at him, pulsing, breathing, then lowered her head. Clicking her beak, she fluttered from his palm onto his shoulder, squeezing his coat in her talons. She allowed the Collector to carry her down again to the ground.

By the time the Collector's boots hit bottom, the starlings had fallen once more into sleep. Water cascaded off the gnarled roots of the oak tree, waterlogging the grass, making it squish. Thunder cracked somewhere overhead.

"Let's go." The Collector skimmed over the oak tree's

roots toward the edge of the clearing, his posture straight and stiff as a post. "Let's go to whoever needs us."

Caladrius said nothing, but he could feel her claws tense. Something whispered behind them. The Collector turned and lifted the Jar of Lights, throwing its blue light into the darkness.

There it was: a body slithering face down along the ground, like a predator crouching in tall grass. The Collector's muscles seized—the creature from the river. This time, his mind couldn't overlay its body with the shape of a fish. It was a man-snake, passing right beside him, sliding beneath the Jar of Lights. He froze agape, staring as it wriggled from tip to tail, searching for something.

"It's looking for her," the Collector said. "The girl from the boat."

The murmuration was forgotten. Something in the Collector's middle felt wrong, as if he were a gear in a machine that had slipped, fallen off its post, and tumbled into darkness.

The monster followed the girl.

The Collector and Caladrius followed the monster.

10

THE SWITCH

ISALINE

The professors held their discussion while Isaline sat on the floor inside the dim examination arena, slumped into a freezing, wet ball. She rubbed her forearms and stared through the Training Center's propped-open door, into the rain and darkness beyond. The sun wouldn't rise for a few hours.

The results of her Weeklong Review were no surprise. Isaline had failed and would have to leave the Academy after sunrise. The examiners were blank-faced and emotionless when they delivered the results; the Headmaster looked so bored he might fall asleep on the spot. He kept half-closing his eyes and drumming his fingers on that stupid clipboard. Isaline wanted to knock it out of his hands.

None of them had believed her about the creature, but that was her own fault. Isaline wouldn't have believed herself either if she had been forced to listen to years of her own excuses. She'd pulled the flare on all her previous Weeklong Reviews, touting cold spells or animal attacks or poisoned berries.

The examiners filed out of the Training Center—the Headmaster grumbling about being exhausted the next day—and left Isaline alone in the examining arena. She took a few bounces on the padded floor and stared at the weapons hanging on hooks, trying to memorize every detail of this place, her favorite spot at the Academy. The trident was hanging on the wall where she had left it. She ran her fingers down its cool metal, her insides shriveling as if she were made of dead leaves.

Outside the building, rain fell in long sweeps. It coated the Training Center's stone steps and spread out onto the pathway below, puddling into a small sea. Isaline spotted the Shute Treasurehunter leaning on the wall outside, watching the water pool below the points of her purple boots.

"That was easy," the Treasurehunter said as Isaline pushed through the door. Her arms were folded, one black-tipped nail drumming on her sleeve.

Isaline ignored her and pounded down the steps into the rain. Casret's large, square courtyard was deserted, dark save for the dimly glowing bulbs of Adrudian lamp-posts. There were a handful of lit windows in the dormitory building up ahead—the few students still studying for their Weeklong Reviews. Isaline hoped Nalissa would be awake like the rest of them.

The Treasurehunter pushed off from the wall and followed Isaline down the walkway. Glancing over her shoulder, Isaline pulled the soaked fabric of her jacket around herself and quickened her pace. The clacking of the Treasurehunter's heels trailed her into the square.

"You must be tired of this." The Treasurehunter's silky voice echoed painfully in Isaline's head. "I know I am."

Isaline tensed her shoulders and kept walking. The dormitory approached, vine-wrapped, cold, and draped in shadows. She imagined herself charging through the dormitory's doors, running up the stairs, and leaving the Treasurehunter alone in the dark. It would feel so good to run away.

"Nalissa," the Treasurehunter said.

Isaline stopped so abruptly she nearly slipped on the wet ground. She whirled. The Treasurehunter's silhouette approached out of the rain.

"What did you say?" Isaline swiped water from her face with her sleeve. "What did you call me?"

The Treasurehunter flashed a lupine grin. She reached into her inside coat pocket, black fingernails disappearing into a swathe of fabric, and pulled out a piece of shiny, stiff paper. It glinted gold in the light of the lamppost shining above them.

"Here." She held the paper out. Isaline took it,

shielding it from the rain with her palm. "Jack went to the station and bought ours yesterday. Everything's good—as long as you can secure that pendant."

Isaline hunched over the paper. It was small, deckled at the edges, and had a shiny gold rectangle of foil in the middle. Stamped over the foil in curling, black script were the words: UPPER TRAIN STATION, THIRD CLASS. TO LOWER TRAIN STATION.

And under the script, written in handwriting: NALISSA.

Isaline's heart jumped against her ribs. She'd never seen a train ticket before. She tried to hold on to reason; maybe there was some kind of mistake.

"Why do—why are you giving this to me?" Raindrops collected like jewels on the gold foil of the ticket. "How ..."

The Treasurehunter had started walking away, crossing over the wet, squelching grass of the courtyard.

Isaline wiped a hand across her eyes. "Hey, wait—"

"Don't pack too much," the Treasurehunter called over her shoulder. Isaline saw the flash of another smile stretching the corners of her mouth. "See you later."

Isaline stood dumbfounded, her feet rooted to the ground. Thunder boomed in the distance. She wanted to run after the Treasurehunter and demand answers, but her legs wouldn't move. What was going on? How did the Treasurehunter know Nalissa? What would Nalissa need with a train ticket?

Numbly, Isaline tucked the ticket into her pocket. She

lurched up the steps to the dormitory, pushed through the heavy oak door, and took the stairs two-at-a-time to her and Nalissa's room. When she reached the right door, she wrapped her fingers around the doorknob and stood there, heart hammering. It felt like a stranger's room.

She pulled the door open.

"Nalissa?"

Darkness and silence inside. Rain pattered on the windowpane between the two beds. Isaline crossed into the room, easing the door closed behind her. She turned the dial on the Adrudian lantern sitting on her writing desk. Orange light bloomed in the dark, bringing the room into focus.

Nalissa's bed was empty and neatly made. Papers were strewn over her desk, the same papers that had half-hidden Isaline's jewelry box two days ago. Isaline turned the dial on the Adrudian lantern until the slats opened as wide as they would go. The room brightened too much, so much it almost hurt.

The truth, she told herself. *You deserve the truth.*

She reached for the papers on Nalissa's desk.

On the top of the pile sat a copy of the Country Watch oath, so pristine it was like Nalissa had never touched it, and a map of the school grounds given to first-year Watchlings. Beneath those were letters from someone in the city. At first glance, the content of the letters made no sense to Isaline: *mill; mines; Listening Spider; House of Matchsticks.* She tossed the letters onto the desk.

Next was a copy of the rules for the Weeklong Review. In red ink, Nalissa had underlined the words: *If a student fails to pass both portions of the exam, they will be expelled from the Academy until further notice.* Isaline stared at the underlined words. She set the paper down on top of the others.

There were two documents left, both folded into separate envelopes. The first envelope was unaddressed and unsealed—a letter that Nalissa had written but hadn't sent. Isaline paused. Was she really going to look at Nalissa's letters? The thought made her heart twist, but she didn't see another option. The other papers had told her nothing.

With clumsy hands, Isaline tugged the paper inside of the envelope out onto her palm. The letter was loosely folded; its ends unfurled on her hand like the petals of a white flower.

Isaline took one look at the words there, written in Nalissa's handwriting, and dropped the paper to the floor as if it had burned her fingers.

Jame, Nalissa had written.

See you soon.

Isaline's mouth went dry as parchment. She turned the last envelope over. It was ripped open and addressed to Nalissa. Slowly, in a dream-like state, she pulled the letter out, nudging open a thick, official-looking cream-colored paper. On it, she read:

You have been summoned to Ar on official Quandary business. Please arrive in the city at two weeks past ...

Isaline let the paper fall from her fingers. Nalissa, in the Quandary? Her best friend? It wasn't real. It had to be a joke.

Sinking, Isaline lowered herself to her bed and buried her bruised face in her hands. Nalissa *had* been hiding secrets from her. She *had* been making plans. Plans to steal ...

My pendant.

Isaline pulled the chain over her head. She held the pendant up in front of her face, peering at the glittering red stone. Hadn't her pendant been at the heart of everything? Hadn't Nalissa tried to steal it? Hadn't that creature tried to kill her for it?

The door to the room swung open. Isaline jumped and the necklace fell out of her hands. The pendant hit the wooden floor and slid, coming up against the toe of Nalissa's boot.

"Oh, hi," Nalissa said. She was wearing her nightclothes, even though she'd been out. Her hair hung loose, falling over her shoulders. "I guess that's it for the Survival Portion, huh?" She bent down to pick up the pendant.

"*No!*" Isaline yelled, launching herself forward and seizing the necklace from Nalissa's hands.

"Wait—what?" Nalissa gaped as Isaline tucked the pendant under her collar. "What's going ..." Her eyes flicked to the floor, where her letters were scattered about, and then to her writing desk, where her papers were toppling over in a pile. The blood in her cheeks drained away.

"Oh, no." Nalissa's voice was barely a whisper. "Oh, no."

ISALINE SLUMPED AGAINST THE WALL, her limbs heavy and exhausted. She and Nalissa had stared at each other, unable to speak, until one of them had shifted onto their bed and crossed their legs, signaling they were ready to talk. Isaline couldn't remember whether it had been her or Nalissa. All she knew was that they had started talking.

"I was found and adopted into the Quandary," Nalissa said. She tapped her fingers, nervous and trying to hide it—but maybe even that gesture had been an act. "That isn't always how it works, but that's the way it worked for me. They trained me to be ... a *spy*." She cringed, as if saying the word out loud to Isaline hurt. "I said yes. They sent me here."

Isaline's face was hot. She spoke downward, straight into the coverlet beneath her legs. "I thought ... I thought we were friends. You never told me."

"The Watch and the Quandary hate each other. At Casret we're ... you're taught to hate Quandary Thieves." Nalissa looked up at Isaline, eyes round. "If I had told you, would you really have kept that secret?"

"I ..." Isaline didn't know the answer. She shook her head. "It doesn't matter now. You've been called away." She pointed to the letter from the Quandary, still on the floor where she'd dropped it. "Were you going to just leave while I was on my exam? Disappear?"

"No," Nalissa said quickly. "I wouldn't." She stood and grabbed the Quandary's letter, then threw it aside onto her writing desk. "This is just my official summons. My leaving has been planned for weeks ... we set it up so that I could get away from the Academy quietly." Her expression was earnest as she held up the stack of letters. "This man—the man who wrote to me, his name is Cameron—he sent his friends to help me fail my Week-long Review. I'm to be expelled, that's it."

"You mean you're going to fail on purpose."

"Exactly." Nalissa leaned against the desk. "I never wanted you to know. I ... I wanted to be your friend, like always."

A lump formed in the back of Isaline's throat. She swallowed, pulling the pendant out of the front of her shirt. "Why were you looking for this, then? And don't lie to me—I noticed my jewelry box missing the night before my exam."

Nalissa chewed her lip, staring at the pendant as it spun in the air. "That pendant ... it's why I was summoned in the first place. I'm supposed to bring it with me. The people who sent for me—they were looking for a red pendant with a keyhole cutout at Casret Academy. It was just by coincidence that my roommate happened to have it. My best friend." Her eyes grew shiny. "I've been struggling with it for weeks. I don't want to take it from you, Isaline."

Isaline pursed her lips. Jame had said something similar, hadn't he? The difference was that he *hadn't* taken it. The real liar had been sitting in Isaline's dorm room all along.

"I met your pen pal in the forest, by the way." Isaline nodded to the pile of letters on the floor. "He said he'd been sending mail to someone at the Academy. He thought he'd meet you on your exam this week."

"Jameson." Nalissa wiped a hand down her face. "I thought he might come through Academy grounds. For someone so brilliant, he can really be stupid."

Isaline didn't want to ask, but the question came bursting out on its own. "Do you ... know him really well?"

"Not beyond his reputation. And a couple of letters," Nalissa said. She sighed at the look Isaline gave her. "He's meeting the same people I am, in the city. In Ar. But I don't like him the same way he likes me. I was just at Marik Taylor's room—we made plans to see each other after graduation."

Isaline had been saving some of her best jokes for this news. Shame she would never get to use them.

"Well, you should be proud of Marik's observational skills, for once," she said. "His monster turned out to be real. Another one of your friends, maybe. It tried to steal my pendant, and kill me, too."

Nalissa's mouth fell open. "The monster was *real?*" She reached across the space between them and took Isaline's hands, forgetting for a moment they were fighting. "I knew you should have rescheduled. I heard there was someone else looking for the pendant ... someone dangerous. But I didn't think they would send an actual *monster*." She shook her head, hair falling into her eyes. "And here I was, worrying about the super-strong clockwork I'm going to have to fight."

Isaline blinked. She yanked her hands back. "Strong clockwork? What strong clockwork?"

Nalissa shrugged, leaning back again. "That's how I'm going to get expelled. Cameron's friend is going to switch the usual sparring clockwork with the strongest at the Academy. I'll get beat up, but at least it'll be convincing." Isaline sat up straighter, but she didn't seem to notice. "The Headmaster won't be able to tell."

Isaline opened her mouth, then closed it again. She stared at the blackened windowpane, not really seeing the raindrops coursing down the glass.

There had been a moment at her Weapons Portion—a split second where the Shute Treasurehunter had given her an unreadable look. How had Isaline interpreted it? A small smile, a twinkle in her eye, like two people sharing a secret? An inside joke?

Nalissa waved a hand in front of Isaline's face. "Isaline? What is it?"

Isaline closed her eyes, trying to recall the Weapons Portion. The Headmaster had scratched something out on his clipboard. He had said, *I have Country Watch listed here.*

The coverlet wrinkled beneath Isaline's clutching hand. She squeezed it so hard the bones in her fingers cracked.

Did anyone call me "Isaline"? Did I tell anyone my name?

"You're scaring me," said Nalissa, "more than usual, here."

"I—I fought a really strong clockwork during my Weapons Portion," Isaline said. "I failed, and—and a stranger was there, on my examining committee." Her mind was spiraling like water down a drain. She reached into her pocket and produced the train ticket. "She gave me this tonight."

Nalissa took the ticket, her eyes widening. "Why would she give this to you? Someone was supposed to bring it to me after I had pulled the flare. But ..." She froze, then lifted her head to meet Isaline's eyes. "Oh, stars. They think you're me. They have us mixed up."

Isaline's breath rushed out of her lungs. "We switched weeks, didn't we? We switched." And they looked alike. Nalissa's hair was wavy to Isaline's curls, and Nalissa's skin and eyes were a tad warmer in tone, but they resembled each other.

She didn't remember standing up off the bed, but suddenly she was on her feet. "You have to tell the Headmaster. I could take the Weapons Portion again."

Nalissa caught her hand, holding her back. "No, Isaline, we tell him, and he'll figure out everything." She dug her fingertips into Isaline's palm. "We can't say anything—we'll just find the person who gave you that ticket and—*Isaline, don't*!"

Isaline pulled Nalissa to the door. Her vision was pulsing as if someone had turned her upside down and shaken her. "We have to tell him," she said, gripping the doorknob. "He'll never believe me, but he'll believe you. I could still be a City Watch. I wouldn't have to go out on my own. Nothing has to change."

Nalissa's face crumpled, her eyes shining like glass marbles. "But everything *has* changed."

"No." Isaline squared her shoulders and pulled the door open. "No, it can't—"

Her sentence died on her lips. There was something waiting for her on the other side of the door.

A white, shivering thing. Pressed into the doorway, inches from Isaline's face. Grinning, head lolling. Slime dripping from its skin onto the floor.

It was the man-snake.

Every nerve in Isaline's body ignited. She went hurtling back, releasing Nalissa's hand and crashing into her writing desk, knocking the Adrudian lantern over on its side. The creature had heaved itself up on its lower half, its spindly arms pressed to the doorframe, supporting its dangling torso. How long had it been there, squeezed against the other side of the door?

"What is that thing?" Nalissa grabbed Isaline's hand and pulled her deeper into the room.

The creature smiled, its wide mouth dripping a line of red-orange ooze below its writhing blindfold. Isaline glanced around the room, looking for a weapon she could use. There was nothing. Her stomach turned over. The room was so small, and the creature was so *big*—she couldn't fight it, not in here. They wouldn't even be able to get around it.

Nalissa set one hand on the top of Isaline's bed, fingers bunching as the creature leaned into the room. It drooped its head to the side as if its neck were made of rubber.

"*Give me the lock,*" it said. Rotting breath blew through the doorway. Isaline and Nalissa sank back in revulsion. "*If you do, I will kill you mercifully.*"

"It's speaking in my head," Nalissa said, clapping her hands over her ears. "Isaline, how is it speaking in my head?"

Isaline's knees locked. There was no way to properly respond. This creature had come for her—she had never dreamed it would follow her into the Academy, but here it was—and she wasn't going to get away so easily this time. The flaps of skin at the hollow of its throat waved in and out, empty. Isaline covered her chest with her palm, pressing the cold lump of the pendant beneath her river-soaked shirt.

The creature slowly moved inside the room. "*Give me the lock.*" Letting out a long, low sound, like moist wind seeping through the rafters of an old house, it lowered itself to the floor, head hanging.

Isaline's mind spun, trying and failing to strategize. They could try to leap over it and escape through the door, but she wasn't sure they could outrun it. Worse, this level of the dormitory was empty; she and Nalissa were the last on their floor to do their Weeklong Reviews, and the building was made of thick stone. No one would hear them, even if they yelled, and their room was too high to jump from the window. They'd have to get down the stairs and into the courtyard before they could find any help.

The creature took its time spreading onto the floor, its long tail-end uncurling. It knew it had them cornered—no reason to rush. Isaline looked around again, to no avail. They had precious little time to find a way to save themselves.

Nalissa touched Isaline's shoulder. "Remember last year, when a rat got caught in our room?"

Isaline pulled her eyes from the creature to look at Nalissa in disbelief. "This thing is bigger than a rat."

"No time to argue," Nalissa said, hoisting the coverlet off her bed and climbing on top of the mattress.

She was right—there wasn't much choice. Isaline climbed onto the other bed and Nalissa tossed the free end of the coverlet toward her. They held it open between them like a net, stretched over the floorspace between the two beds. Isaline fought to keep her arms still. This was never going to work. Even if they could catch it, what would they do?

The creature slid toward them, unhurried. The skin of its face squeaked along the floor.

Nalissa made eye contact with Isaline over the blanket. Time slowed. For a moment, Isaline forgot Nalissa was a spy for the Quandary of Thieves. They were Watchlings again, catching a rat.

Wait, Nalissa mouthed.

The creature crept closer.

Wait, Isaline mouthed back, in time with Nalissa.

Wait.

It rushed between them.

Now.

With twin cries, Isaline and Nalissa threw the coverlet over the creature. It let out a low screech and started thrashing, limbs punching beneath the fabric.

"Isaline! The lantern!" Nalissa yelled.

Isaline leaped to the foot of her bed, slipping on the exposed sheets over her mattress and windmilling her arms. She grabbed the shining Adrudian lantern from the writing desk and held it up by its wire handle, a tiny orange sun. Her eyes strained as she tried to pick out which flailing lump under the coverlet was the monster's head.

"Here!" Nalissa gestured with her arm.

Isaline swung the lantern downward, putting all the force she could behind it. There was an ear-splitting *crack* as its impact on the creature shattered the glass. The slats in the lantern slid closed and its frame broke into pieces, stifling the light.

Darkness swept in. The flailing body underneath the coverlet went still.

Isaline glanced at Nalissa, or tried to; she couldn't see her hand in front of her face. A silent second went by, then another. The monster didn't move. Isaline's eyes adjusted to the thin light, and Nalissa's outline swam out of the dark, silhouetted by the smooth panes of the window. Rain beat against the glass in sheets.

"Is ... is it dead?" Nalissa moved to lift up the coverlet, but thought better of it. "Good thing we didn't try that lantern trick with the rat."

Despite her trembling knees, Isaline found herself laughing. "You wouldn't have slept for a week."

Nalissa laughed, too. "I wouldn't have slept ever again. We should—"

Her sentence stopped short. With a roar—not a screech or hiss this time, but an actual *roar*—the monster came to life again, heaving beneath the coverlet.

Isaline gasped, sucking air into her lungs. The monster jolted upwards. Crying out, Nalissa ran across the mattress toward the door, stumbling over her writing desk and sending papers flying. The monster swiveled and reached out with flexing fingers, making a bizarre, deranged hissing noise. Its hands closed around Nalissa's ankles and pulled her off the writing desk and to the floor.

Isaline went cold. As Nalissa flung herself against the wall, scrambling to get away, Isaline charged toward the creature. But it was ready. It reached behind its back with one hand and shoved her with remarkable strength. She went stumbling across the room and cannoned into the frame of Nalissa's bed.

Pain shot through Isaline's hips, turning her vision fuzzy. The creature raised its arms from the ground at its side, its body bending at the waist, arcing up horribly like a snake. Nalissa's lips thinned against her teeth, a mask of fear. The creature reached its long fingers to the back of its head, feeling over its patchy scalp toward the knot of its blindfold.

"*No!*" Isaline cried, and reached out to hit it, pull it, *anything* to keep it from taking that blindfold off. But the shock of falling on the bed frame had made her dizzy—she couldn't get up in time.

The knot untied and the blindfold fell around the creature's shoulders. Lightning flashed, bathing the room in white light so cold it chilled Isaline to her core. Nalissa's gaze lifted up, up—it seemed to take forever—and clamped onto the monster's squirming eyes.

Isaline struggled against the floor as Nalissa's mouth widened. Her face went stony, and even as the room sank again into darkness, Isaline could see her cheeks draining of color. Nalissa's arms fell one after the other from their position in mid-air, *pat-pat* on the floor. Her shoulders drooped. Her head slumped against the wall.

She was dead.

A crater opened up in Isaline's chest. Her awareness was jerked out of her body, and she numbed, dissociated, being lifted up, up on a wave. There was a muffled sliding sound as Nalissa's body slipped down the wall. Isaline saw the creature swivel toward her as if from above, its blindfold tumbling down its back and sticking on its dripping gash.

It came forward, slowly, and a fresh jolt of adrenaline set Isaline's limbs on fire. In a wild panic, she clamped a hand over her eyes. She felt around for the edge of Nalissa's bed and tried to stand up.

"Leave me alone!" Her voice came out a wheeze. "Get away from me! You killed her!"

The creature made a loud hissing sound. *"Give me the lock."* Its voice slid into her ears like water, drowning out everything around it. *"Give it to me, girl."*

Isaline slapped her hand over her chest where the pendant lay buried in the fabric of her shirt. She pressed her other palm over her eyes hard enough to flatten her eyelids. "No. *No no no no no!*"

"Dead girl …" the creature breathed, heedless of her screaming. *"I will take it."*

Isaline pushed herself backward onto Nalissa's bed and shuffled until her back hit the wall. She was operating purely on instinct; in the back of her mind, she knew there was no way out of this. Not with one hand over her eyes, not with her best friend dead at the foot of her bed, not with their floor empty of students. No one was coming to help.

The end of the bed depressed under the creature's weight. It was slithering toward her. Her body shuddered. The hand she had clamped over her eyes was trembling so violently she had to fight to keep it from leaping off.

"The House of Matchsticks will accept your sacrifice," the creature said.

Isaline opened her mouth to answer—or maybe to scream, whatever happened first—but she didn't have a chance. An ear-piercing *boom* suddenly resounded from across the room.

The weight on the end of the bed shifted. A pair of boots, or maybe two, stomped into the room. Isaline's heart pounded so hard she felt her ribs were going to break.

"There!" a familiar voice shouted.

Footsteps came bounding toward her. There was a quick snap of light—too short and bright to be lightning—followed by a fizzing noise.

"Don't look at the eyes!" the same voice said.

The mattress sprung up as the weight on the end was pulled off. The creature roared. Isaline was frozen to the spot, her breaths coming in gasps. She didn't dare peel her hand away from her eyes.

Boots barreled all over the room. They came up in the space between the two beds, and the creature screeched, close to Isaline's side. She shrank into the corner.

The voice grunted, lifting something heavy. "Off —you—go."

A sudden, deafening crash made Isaline jerk and hit her head on the wall. The sound of wailing wind intensified, followed by a spray of cold water. Isaline gasped in a lungful of rain-scented air and curled herself up, bringing her knees into her chest.

The pair of boots turned and came toward her.

"Open your eyes." The voice was loud over the howling of the wind. "It's gone."

Isaline lifted her hand from her face. The figure of a woman swam in front of her eyes. A long, black braid swung over her shoulder and into the crook of her arm.

The Shute Treasurehunter.

"I tossed it out the window," The Treasurehunter said, "but it'll be back. Never thought it would follow you in here. We have to move."

Isaline could only gape. The door to the room had been flung open, and at the threshold stood the silhouette of a man she didn't recognize. He had a dark jacket buttoned up around his neck and stood with rigid posture, looking down the hallway with one hand on the doorknob. He glanced into the room.

"Come on," he said. "Let's go."

The Treasurehunter looked at him over her shoulder. "Give her a minute." She turned to Isaline. "Can you stand?"

Isaline wasn't sure if she could. The numbness was coming back, turning her legs to bags of water. She had one hand clutched to her chest over the red pendant. It rose and fell rabbit-quick with her breathing.

"M-my friend ..." she said. "She's ... is she—"

The Shute Treasurehunter nodded. "Unfortunately. I'm sorry."

"Come on," the man at the door said. His voice was gruff, low, as if he'd swallowed a toad. Isaline couldn't see his face—the light from the hallway was too bright, and besides, his features were hidden in a mass of tangly black hair.

Isaline toed the ground, her boots squelching on the wooden floor. The Treasurehunter held out a hand to help her.

"Do you have other boots?" she asked. "Those ones look ..." She stared at Isaline's feet as if the Survival Portion boots could reach out and bite her. "Wet."

Isaline nodded silently and stood up. Her legs wobbled, but somehow, they supported her. She released the Treasurehunter's hand and pointed at a pair of boots sitting near the doorway. They weren't Isaline's, but Nalissa never minded if Isaline borrowed her shoes—they were the same size.

"Great." The man at the door stooped to swipe the boots off the ground. "We don't have time for this."

Isaline looked over her shoulder at the window. It wasn't a window anymore, just a crunch of broken glass with a jagged hole in the middle. The sill and the floor beneath it were coated in glistening rain.

"Not the quiet exit we had hoped for," the Shute Treasurehunter said. She placed a hand on Isaline's back and guided her gently toward the door. "But there's no use in waiting now."

Nalissa's body came into view beyond her writing desk. She was lying where the creature left her, slumped against the wall. The man with the jacket must have covered her with the fallen blanket, because she was now just a jumble of limbs under gray fabric. The hole in Isaline's chest expanded and out-of-body terror threatened to overtake her again. Her legs started to give out beneath her; she clutched the side of one of the desks, fighting to stay upright.

"My name is Neave," the Shute Treasurehunter said in her ear. "It's nice to meet you for real, finally. My friend here is Jack."

The man looked their way. His jaw was dusted with a prickly black beard and framed by a dark mustache. With a start, Isaline noticed bluish-purple veins creeping up from beneath the collar of his jacket, spiderwebbing his white skin from jawline to temple.

What were people who drank Adrudian Milk called? She couldn't remember. Her mind was a thick soup.

"We were coming to get you. Heard the commotion." Neave looked at the shattered window. "Persistent, isn't it, that thing?" She let go of Isaline's shoulders and placed her hands at her hips. For the first time, Isaline noticed she was wearing a full weapons belt, complete with a shiny, square Flash Camera. "Do you have the pendant?"

Isaline pressed her hand over her chest, where the necklace was tucked into her shirt.

Neave gave her a confident smile. "Good. Let's go. That thing will be back any minute, and we don't have much time to catch the train."

She strode toward the door. Isaline didn't move to follow her.

"I ..."

Tell them. Tell them you're just a Watchling. Tell them you're not Nalissa.

But the words wouldn't come. Isaline's lungs were as tight as two iron cages. They couldn't possibly believe her, and the Headmaster would never listen to her. The only person he would have listened to was ...

She couldn't form the thought. Isaline could barely force herself to look at the gray coverlet with the lumps underneath. One of Nalissa's hands was sticking out from under the edge, fingers curled into a fist. Isaline sank to her knees.

But everything has *changed.*

She touched Nalissa's curled-up fist. It felt like a stranger's hand. What kind of life had Nalissa lived? Who had she talked to—what had she done? Tears rolled down Isaline's face.

I can't stay at the Academy without you. I can't leave. I'll never make it on my own. Tell me what to do, Nalissa. Tell me—

Something was clutched in Nalissa's fist. A paper. Dazed, Isaline pulled it from Nalissa's hand and smoothed it out on the top of her thigh. Gold foil glinted in the light.

UPPER TRAIN STATION, THIRD CLASS. TO LOWER TRAIN STATION.

NALISSA.

In that moment, Isaline imagined she heard an audible *click,* like the grind of a railroad switch, sending a speeding train off its path and over a new, strange set of tracks.

A voice cut through the stillness. It wasn't the Shute Treasurehunter, but the man, Jack, who spoke.

"What was her name?" he asked, looking at Nalissa.

Numbly, Isaline squeezed Nalissa's hand, then stood and slid the train ticket into the breast pocket of her jacket. It sat, still warm, against her chest.

"Isaline," she said. "Her name was Isaline."

THE ADVENTURE CONTINUES IN ...

PART TWO OF THE HOUSE OF MATCHSTICKS SERIES

Discover the next leg of the journey at elisadowning.com.

WANT FREE HOUSE OF MATCHSTICKS CONTENT?

Hi! Elisa here.

I hope you enjoyed *House of Matchsticks* (Part 1). If you did, I'd love to hear from you in a review. Reviews help readers take notice of books—and even a sentence or two can mean the world to indie authors like myself. Thank you so much!

If you're itching to read more House of Matchsticks content, join my newsletter to receive your free House of Matchsticks Reader Bundle. You'll get a novelette starring Jack and Cameron, map downloads, and more. Find out more at my website: elisadowning.com.

As always, thank you for reading. And see you in the House of Matchsticks.

ELISA DOWNING

THE HOUSE OF MATCHSTICKS SERIES

House of Matchsticks
Night of Matchsticks
Tree of Matchsticks

ALSO BY ELISA DOWNING

Josie and the Scary Snapper

ABOUT THE AUTHOR

Elisa Downing is an author of strange stories about brave kids, teens, and new adults. An MA Children's Literature graduate, she's spent years climbing through the windows of books to better see the world beyond. She enjoys writing fantastical adventures full of ancient mysteries, slow-burn romance, and lots of monsters. When she's not writing, you can find Elisa reading under a tree somewhere, playing video games on easy mode, waxing poetic over cult cinema, or watching horror movies.

www.ingramcontent.com/pod-product-compliance
Lightning Source LLC
Chambersburg PA
CBHW030338310726
48979CB00001B/85

* 9 7 8 1 7 7 7 8 8 5 7 1 7 *